The Last Throne

A Novel

Tristen Davis

The Library of Congress has cataloged

this book as follows:

Name: Tristen Davis

Title: The Last Throne

Subject: Young Adult Fantasy

ISBN: 9798463279033

To my husband who is always in the stands, to my mom who inspired me to read, and to the village that got me here.

Chapter 1

"They're all dead; their bodies were found outside the Tangled Forest."

I sip my ale as I eavesdrop on the men sitting at the table behind us. I look up from my frosted glass when I feel Lilliana's heart, next to me, racing. We'd chosen this spot for its anonymity; travelers from all over come here to get drunk and go home with someone new. I inhale the familiar mix of stale ale and regrets as the band lulls me into its rhythm. As our shoulders touch, I look over to Lilliana and offer her my famous smile. She is always nervous about us getting caught here, or worse, killed. Our itchy black robes chafe against our arms and legs as we overhear the disturbing conservation. I listen closely for their heartbeats, each one of them calls to me, and they thump slowly in their bodies, succumbing to the amount of liquor they have enjoyed this evening. I couldn't do much with that feeling though, Lilliana's elbow welcomed me with a jab, and I let go, relaxing in my seat.

We continue to listen to their conversation and gather that they are service guards. I imagine their robes each flashing the designated colors according to which element they could break; ever since the invasions from Naluen, they have been scattered throughout the kingdom to serve different posts and to warn the nobles of any incoming attacks. What the guards witnessed regularly, what they had to do to keep the kingdom safe, often led them to drink here with us on nights like these.

"Emma." Her elbow greets my side again as she whispers, "We should go."

I hear the creak of her chair as it turns. My own feet hit the ground with a thud; my stolen black boots feel heavy against the plank flooring. The view of the men behind us becomes more apparent as we pass, and I notice their loose robes hanging off them; table littered with empty mugs. Even off duty, I know not to mess with them. It would be game over if anyone recognized me, and the Marquess would make sure I never left the Summer Palace again. Hidden beneath the dark cloak and the maid's uniform we stole from the kitchens, the cool hilt of a small dagger clings to the outside of my thigh. I'd found it discarded in a pile of supplies to be burned and snatched it before it could be carried off in the trash. Its blade was slightly dull and gray, and the handle was carved wood that fit the previous owners' hand well. I may be in the process of doing something completely reckless and inappropriate, but I'm not naïve enough to enter the pub empty-handed.

"Well, would you look at the pretty girl here." The youngest guard wears an orange robe, BlazeBreaker, I think to myself. He reaches out to touch Lilliana, and his hard-edged face shines under the candlelight. I was wrong in assuming we could pass by unnoticed.

"Leave her alone!" I press forward, grab Lilliana's arm, and tug her along out of his reach. His hands grasp my robe, and I shove his arm backward; he lands in his seat with a thud.

"Maybe she doesn't want to be with you," he replies as he struggles to get up from his chair and follows us drunkenly through the pub.

Anxiety surfaces as I look back at the other guards and size them up. I'm decent at defending myself, but I can't take them all down. Forcing the muscles along my body to ease, I keep walking towards the large double door with Lilliana pulling me along; I reply, "We were just on our way."

The other guards follow behind us, tailing us as we navigate the mismatched wooden tables throughout the large room. As I inch closer to the door, heat erupts around us; I smell the burnt hairs of my cloak in the air. Screams echo throughout the room as chaos erupts in all directions. The wind that hits our backs knocks us to the ground. As I look up, one of the guards slams into the wall with a sickening crack. I feel the dagger's hilt in my hands as I ensure my hood is still covering my head. Another one of the guards, the younger one, presses forward. His frame is slightly bigger than mine, and he reeks of ale and sweat.

"You must not have heard me." He lifts his arms with ease, and my face burns from the flames that surround us. As I try to connect with my breaking and pull from his energy, I lift my arms and sway them as a light breeze rustles through the room. The chaos around us is unleashed as tables and chairs enter the air, shooting past us.

He continues to stare and smiles at me with a crooked grin. Shit, I think, I am going to have to do this the old fashion way. As I rise, my feet hit the floor, and the back of my robe is yanked through the doorway behind me and out into the moonlit night. The cool air whips my robe around me and threatens to pull back my hood. I feel Lilliana behind me, attempting to drag me away, as I stare at the BlazeBreaker in front of me. He stumbles closer, hands facing outwards, ready to let his flames consume us. As I wiggle free from her grasp, aware of my singed robes, my heart slows, and I let my hand slip into the slit along the side of the uniform. My fingers close around the smooth wooden hilt of the dagger. I don't care who this man is; no one is going to threaten me, not in my kingdom.

"Us three can have some fun." He smiles at us as the flames surround us again, inching closer. Lilliana's scream stings my ears as she presses into my back.

I shoot forward, dipping under his arms; my robe burns lazily as the smoke enters my lungs. I spring up behind him, fisting the back of his robes, and thrust the dagger into his back, the way Commander Kirk had taught me.

He yelps in pain as he flails wildly, the flames around us dying as he loses control. He writhes and attempts to retrieve the dagger from his back, screaming at the other guards approaching. His roar sends my instincts into overdrive as we run for it; I feel my boots slipping on the wet stones as they move faster than we can process. Feeling their racing heartbeats behind us, we dive forward. The wooden boards of a wagon greet my face as I land and make impact. Silence is all that welcomes us as we await the destruction of the guards ripping us from the wagon or burning it down with us inside. The wagon rustles with movement; I call out to Liliana to stop moving and notice that we are swaying back and forth. Peeking over the side, I see the moonlit stones passing by, and I lay back, releasing a heavy breath; I feel through my cloak for my dagger and pat my robe.

"It's gone!" My hands clutch my cheeks. "I lost my dagger in the back of that guard."

"Well, we can't go back. We have to make it back soon, or else the Marchioness will figure out we were gone." Lilliana says fearfully as she leans forward and dusts herself off.

"I know a way; we have to get off by the town square and then take the east side servant's entrance, through the kitchens," I answer as the tightness of her hand squeezes mine. After a while, we measure our distance and silently scoot off the back of the wagon as it passes the east entrance to the

Summer Palace. Sticking to the shadows, robes covering us, we

make our way into the palace.

Chapter 2

After having breakfast with the Marchioness, I sneak out to the east garden. Ensuring that nobody is watching me, I move like a ghost through the palace. There is no view of this side of the garden from the palace, and it's where I practice breaking the elements between the tall hedges. I ready myself and feel the elements around me; I don't have to try too hard. Being out here is overwhelming as they won't let me ignore them. My breathing falters as I hear my name being called again and look around to see who is yelling, "Emma!"

I recognize her voice as she marches along, the pea gravel crunching underneath her black leather riding boots. The glow of the morning sun blinds us as it washes through the garden, casting us in an orb of golden light. Large white roses reflect pearlescent as the light catches them and surrounds her. Roses cover the area this time of year in preparation for the moon festival. This is one of my favorite places to be in the entire Summer Palace, my home.

"I'm over here!" I call to Lilliana as soon as she notices me. I try to focus again, deep breath in, allowing myself to feel the wind around me. I lift my arms as I maintain my hold on it, begging it to break and do as I command. I let my arms down as it settles around me, blowing the stray dead leaves off the bushes in front of me.

Pulling myself from my concentration, the ground rumbles beneath my feet, and I listen. It's hard to focus with each element begging you for your attention. I dig my toes deeper into the gravel until I hit the soil below with my bare feet. The world around me teases me as it exists but refuses my will. I lose myself in the vibrations I detect with my toes, still dug into the soil. Breathing deep, the sun embraces my face as it peeps through the clouds and injects warmth into my skin.

14

"Lilli, do you feel that?" My eyes are closed against the bright light of day, the sun heats my skin, and I can feel a slight tingling, not enough to burn, but I know that I will be a little more tan by tomorrow.

"Feel what?" she replies, her tone abrupt.

Her heartbeat echoes with a thump that shakes my muscles as she approaches. Feeling that she is getting closer, I open my eyes, her arms still hugging the colorful stack of books she always carries. We both love to read; I secretly hope she found some for me as well this time. The wind picks up again as I attempt to break it, grabbing hold of it with the upwards lift of my arms. The gust surrounds us both. Our dresses whip frantically around our legs, and the bushes surrounding us chime in unison as the wind sweeps through them. My hair lashes my face, obscuring my vision and sticking to the edges of my lips. My concentration falters as the ground rumbles again; the breeze that pressed fiercely into my skin was dying. Dust settles as it paints the nearby rose bushes with a reddish-brown coating.

Feeling defeated, the bench greets me with a cool touch beneath my dress. "I feel this rumbling." I sigh heavily. "It's vibrating the bones in my feet."

"Don't worry too much, Em." Lilliana retorts. She is right. I do worry often, and it consumes my thoughts and keeps me up at night.

"You're right; I shouldn't worry, it's just—"

One moment I am looking at Lilli, beautiful, the next, I'm on my back, blinded by what has knocked me off the bench. The ground rumbles below us as it shakes me entirely, my brain rattling against the inside of my skull.

Disoriented, I hear screaming, and it sounds like Lilli; I struggle to get up as the world is turned on its head, and I can't tell which way I should be going. In no time, I see service guards rush to the garden and surround us. Each of them is in their uniforms and color-coded for their breaking ability. The guards approaching us wear white robes with silver-plated armor poking out the sides. They are WindBreakers; they can control the wind and manipulate it to their will. I feel the vibrations getting stronger as I look down to notice the soil splitting and shifting, cracks forming among the garden path of pea gravel.

GroundBreakers! I think to myself as I get to my feet and search for Lilli. I spot her on her side by the bench where we were sitting; her body bent at an awkward angle. The rocks poke and tear into me as I crawl to her. Crumbling around us, pieces of stone from the bench are lifted into the air and shot across the garden at incoming service guards. The gust from the WindBreakers forces me to lower myself next to Lilli, arms shaking; I pull her body along the path out of the way.

The service guards scream plans and orders to stop the intruders. "HELP!" I struggle as I attempt to lift Lilli's body. I notice blood seeping from under her head where it lays in my lap. I don't feel any movement from her, and it scares me.

Tears stream down my face and burn my eyes; I rub them with the sleeve of my black dress. I try to feel the wind and land around me, hands trembling; the wind and dirt are a constant in my bones, but they refuse to listen to my command. I lift my arms as the vibrations get more substantial, and I feel myself grab ahold of it; blinded by the pain, I lose my hold, and it fizzles around me. My scalp burns hot as my head snaps back and my feet lift off the ground. A man, navy uniform with intricate gold detailing, stares back at me with a toothy grin.

"Naluen! Soldiers from Naluen!" I scream! My vision distorts as his fist connects with my jaw. My arms go up instinctively, and I kick out at him; my foot hits something substantial as he lets out a whimper.

"I have the Ornae!" he shouts as he attempts to grab me again; sizing him up, I notice the scar above his left eye and his missing teeth. His black hair is sandy as it is cut short to his scalp.

He moves for me, and I duck, avoiding his grasp, I feel through the slit I made in my dress, and my bare thigh confirms my fears. I have no weapon.

My assailant pulls the rocky ground around him and directs it into a sharp point; I stare at the sharp blade he has formed from the soil. He smiles maliciously at me and screams something to the others that I don't understand.

"You either die here, or you come with me, your choice." He winks at me, gold tooth shining in the sunlight. His sword is held out towards me lazily, as if he thinks he has the upper hand.

"I choose neither," I reply quickly, then move towards him and feel the air off his sword as it swipes past me. I slam my hands into his wrist. I twist hard, prying the blade from his grasp. It struggles to maintain its form as I attempt to hold it together; it takes everything inside me. He presses forward and lifts the ground around me. My hands tingle with the soil dissolving from the sword. I twist quickly and thrust the blade into his side with a swipe.

"You little bitch!" he screams as he waves his hands and the sword dissolves into the air. My feet decide my next move for me as they instruct me to retreat. The unevenness intensifies as the gravel shifts; my ears ring with the crackling it sends into the air. Pain shoots up from my foot as the ground swallows it and I drop and bite into the soil. White-hot pain throbs up my leg, and I turn back towards the GroundBreaker. The Naluen soldier stands over me and laughs, "You must not be used to being around GroundBreakers, surprising for an Ornae."

I struggle silently as the ground presses into me, holding me within its tight grip and refusing to let me go. It constricts my body faster, and a hoarse gasp for air escapes my throat. The gold detailing on the soldier's uniform scatters the morning sun around him as he steps closer to me. With a wave of his arms, it answers and provides him with a long sword that covers his entire arm, its point solidified. I stare back at it, begging it to break to my command. I look up to notice his halt as he feezes and staggers backward away from me. I shiver as the ground surrounding me releases its grip, and I inhale sharply. I stare cautiously as the attacker crumbles to the ground, blood flooding out of his nose and mouth. His knife dissolves as it hits the dirt, and dust greets my face curiously. I hear more screaming as the service guards approach us.

Took them long enough, I think silently. Commander Kirk lowers his arms from behind my assailant, and I notice the smell of metallic blood that surrounds me. His red robes flap in the breeze as he approaches and lifts me from the ground.

"Emma, Are you okay?" he asks, the sun reflecting off his bald umber toned scalp.

"I'm fine; he didn't hurt me. Where is Lilli?" I dust myself off and notice the rush of guards still moving throughout the garden.

"We are still looking and making sure everyone is accounted for." He has a look of discernment in his eyes. I know that look; I've seen a lot of it lately, with threats arriving from other countries about my upcoming ritual. He won't tell me the truth, what is going on with the other countries that have recently attempted to invade Nadeem.

We have been at war with them since I was born. However, they are now getting braver. I have been collecting information using the servants' quarters adjacent to his office; slipping slightly into a linen closet, I would peer through the grate that allowed air to flow throughout the palace. There were always discussions regarding the countries surrounding Nadeem, Naluen on our west coast, and Navak to our east. Each country has its fair share of Breakers, but they are losing their powers. Commander Kirk had informed the Marquess that the WaveBreakers they had captured during the east invasion from Navak could barely defend themselves. I was shocked to hear of someone losing their ability; here in Nadeem, the

Breakers live long lives, almost immortal; however, I've seen them die. They were strong enough to flatten buildings and capsize large ships. During my Oracle lessons, we discussed why the Great Mother hadn't blessed the other countries with an Ornae. She claimed it was because of nightwalkers inhabiting the other countries, a curse from the Great Mother. It gave them incredible strength and speed, but they were unable to go out in the daylight.

Commander Kirk interrupts my thoughts as he escorts me inside, "They will take you to your chambers, and I want you to remain there until we do a full sweep."

"I have to find her," I argue, staring directly at him.

"We will, but first, we need to get you inside and somewhere safe." He turns his back to me and bellows, "Guards, take the Ornae to her chambers; once secured, report back here for a full sweep of the grounds." They salute him in unison and move towards me,

I know when I've lost, I let them guide me back to my chambers. Heat rises to my face as I fear the worst.

Chapter 3

The gray stone walls of my chambers stare back at me as I lay on my bed, dust assaulting me with each inhalation. The impression my body left in my bed still clings to me, still in my dress, the bits of dirt and dead leaves decorate it. I turn my head back and gaze across the room. The large stack of books stares back at me. Nora often lets the kitchen maids collect books when they are in other rooms of the palace; I had also stolen some myself or gotten them from Lilli. Always making sure the books were put back where they belonged and without getting caught. My room isn't much to gawk at, just a small bed, two chairs placed by the fireplace, a wardrobe, and a chest.

Silence at the door snaps my attention away from my thoughts, and my palms dampen as I glance at the closed door to the hallway. My feet slide across the cold, rough surface of the stone floor and make my way to the door. It creaks like an old bag of bones, and I stare out into the empty hallway. The guards must have reported downstairs for the meeting. No doubt Commander Kirk would be laying into them about the issues they faced when the GroundBreakers had attacked. I hope none of them were seriously injured during the fight. It's not like they had a choice to join the service guard. As a child, they were tested to see if they had any breaking abilities. If they did, they were taken as conscripts of the kingdom to serve and protect as guards.

Stealthily, I keep to the shadows as I pass servants and Nobles on my way across the castle on the same path Lilliana and I had taken as children when we raced up and down the hallways to see who was the fastest. I reach the room where Commander Kirk will be meeting with the guards to go over the details and enter the door on the other side. The dark room is quiet as it greets me with a musty scent. It's a linen closet used by the servants who dress the beds and change the sheets, mainly shelves lining the walls of the room with a table centered in the middle for folding. I lean down under the table and crawl near the grate that connects the rooms. Light peers through the grate and illuminates my face as I hear the door slam into the other room. Commander Kirk comes into view. Leaning closer, I hear another person step forward.

"We haven't found her, my Lord. It seems they must have taken her during their retreat."

Commander Kirk responds to the noble, "What about the lady's maid for the Ornae?" By his hoarse reply, I can tell that it's the Marquess.

"She was also unable to be located," Commander Kirk answers. Anger boils inside of me. They haven't found Lilliana.

The Marchioness enters the room demanding, "How did this happen?" Her jewels securing her brown hair glitter under the candlelight as she paces the room frantically. "How did someone get into the east garden and get that close to us?"

"We are still scouting the area, my Lady. We plan to retaliate accordingly," he murmurs in reply.

"Yes, you will." She slams the door on her exit, and the click of her heels on the stone grows more distant.

The Marques rubs his temples. "Very well, we will have a replacement assigned to the Ornae then. Thank you." With a wave of his hand, he exits the room. A thump sounds as Commander Kirk plops into his chair and throws his red robes over it. My fingers grip the grate until the metal cuts into my skin. My hands scream in pain as I stare forward. I will find out what happened to Lilliana, and if anyone has hurt her, I will kill them.

I exit the linen closet silently and take a deep breath. Tears streak my face as I attempt to not think the worst. The stone grazes against my feet as they drag, and the scent of sweet bread lures me to it as I migrate closer to the kitchens. Pots and pans clink together, and rushing water greets me as I arrive, staring through the large doorway. Three wooden islands stand in the middle of the large kitchen, where maids are chopping viciously. I look over at the fire spreading from the large stones in the wall and the stove where pots boil rapidly. I spot Nora commanding her troops to prepare for this evening's dinner. Red hair escapes her bonnet in every direction. I look around the large kitchen to notice who is working and say hello to everyone as I navigate through the chaos.

Nora motions for me as she dumps boiling water into a large pot on the fire. Clouds of white cover her face and hair, red on her cheeks, and age around her eyes. She greets me with a smile that could make anyone feel at home. "Oh, my dear, are you okay? I heard about the attack in the garden." She stares at me, frightened.

"I'm fine, just rattled." My cheeks heat as the tears streak down my face. Eyes burning, I let down the wall that I had been holding up. I'm not fine. Her arms catch me and hold me tightly as I let myself be carried away in them.

"Oh dear, she will be back," she murmurs as she holds me, my face still crushed into her bosom.

"They still haven't found her. I'm not sure what I'll do if something has happened to her." My body rocks as the sobs escape me. "If I had control of my breaking, none of this would have happened."

"I know, dear. Have you eaten yet? Let me fix you some soup" I hear the dishes clink together as she maneuvers around the kitchen, stirring the contents of a large silver pot.

"I can't eat now, Nora." My eyes itch as I wipe them with my dress.

"I won't hear any more of that. No girl of mine is going to sit and worry on an empty stomach." I hear the soup being poured into the bowl as she bellies up to the counter and places it in front of me. I'm not really her daughter, but the closest thing to it, I think. The other maids had told me she had lost her daughter when she was killed by a mysterious illness at birth. I had never had a mother, though, as I was orphaned by my parents, and Nora had found me and brought me to the Summer Palace.

"This is delicious," I exclaim as my tongue flinches against the steaming broth.

"Thank you, dear, it's my mother's recipe. The Duke and Marquess will have it this afternoon." Wind erupts us as she fans herself with her apron, sweat running from her hair as it runs down to the nape of her neck.

Gods, I thought. "Why is the Duke here?"

"I am not sure, you know how these Nobles are, with no current Voya they have free rein and roam as they please." Her shoulders go up in a shrug as she moves back to cutting potatoes.

Nadeem hasn't had a Voya since the last one had disappeared. I didn't know the Voya personally; it's not like the noble's lineage, many of the noble families passed down the titles to their children, and it's how they managed to keep money and power within the family. The true ruler of the country would be me, the Ornae, and I would become the Voya on my eighteenth birthday. Which was coming up sooner than I was comfortable with.

"That may change one of these days," I state as my spoon scrapes the bottom of my bowl.

"Yes, it may. Until then, I need you to take care of yourself and stay safe. You are going to be a great Voya. I know it. I know your heart." She points to my chest.

"I lost my dagger," I say, exasperated.

"Oh dear, well, maybe it's for the best. Those things are more trouble than they're worth." She wipes the tears from my cheeks, and I nod as she rubs my back with the warmth that only a mother can.

"If the Marquess finds out you can defend yourself, you'll never see the light of day again." The Great Mother never intended for the Voya to be able to defend herself in combat, just to end the war. I shiver as I recall the last time I was locked in my room; I had questioned the Marchioness at a formal dinner. When it came to discussing war and politics, I was expected to be seen, not heard.

"Well, they won't find out." My voice is hoarse and creaky. The kitchen has always been comforting to me. I hang out here most days and discuss gossip with the kitchen staff. It's always fascinating to learn what is going on. The Nobles upstairs never bother with me. The maids have stories from when they go into town and when they encounter other boys and girls on errand runs. I listen to them as we walk the hallways of the palace like I've done since Nora brought me here.

I'm brought back to the present by a rap on the door frame. I turn in my chair as a dark green combat uniform with black armor plating catches my attention as she approaches.

Her black braids twist down each side of her sepia-toned skin,

glowing golden in the sunlight that spills through the doorway.

"Hello, Ornae, I am your new lady's maid, Jasmine."

Chapter 4

We approach the large oak double doors of the lessons room and swing them open, creaking metal rings out.

"I'll be leaving you; I have a meeting with Commander Kirk," Jasmine announces as she waits for me to enter the room. I stare back at her as the door creaks open loudly, and I slip inside.

I look to the front of the classroom and notice the single table in the middle of the room. My seat. I cross the room silently. Feeling eyes on me, I look up and greet the Oracle accordingly. Her silky black robes cover her entirely and her hood allows only her face to be visible for others to see. She moves towards me and plops the books down on the table. I grab the first one off the top and open it.

"Read aloud!" she bellows across the room as I crack it open and begin reciting the text.

"After many years of destruction and war that had decimated the borders, leaving the countryside in ruins, and costing each country thousands of lives. The world was on the brink of chaos. Until the Ornae had stepped forward, mastering each element, and blessed by the Great Mother, she had leveled the field with bodies and ripped the hearts from each of the soldiers."

"How did she achieve this?" Her long gray nail drags along the page in front of me and taps rapidly.

"Through HeartBreaking" I answer abruptly. "The fifth element, the blood that runs through our veins." I take a long deep breath and try to ignore the overwhelming urge to throw the book at her. Its heavy binding would do some damage. Imagining her wounded brings forth a surprising amount of glee.

"Next," the oracle booms.

"The Great Mother blessed the country of Nadeem, the Ornae had ended the war and brought peace to the lands. She ruled over Nadeem as Voya until the next Ornae would be found. To bless the other and spread her gifts, the Voya had allowed others to share her blood."

Except she had disappeared shortly afterwards. They each had disappeared after the rituals of becoming the Voya. A shudder passes through me as I imagine blood pouring from her into the mouths of others.

Lightening quick, she makes her way across the table in the blink of an eye, and her grip tightens around my neck.

"Why did you shudder?" Her salty breath flows around me and makes me nauseous. This isn't the first time I have been reprimanded for speaking out of turn. I was not the Voya yet, so they could do as they pleased.

"You will listen and listen well girl," she seethed between her brown teeth, "that is part of being who you are."

Her grip tightens around my neck as I am confronted with her gray, hardened face.

"It just seems like a lot to ask for. If that's how the Breakers got their powers, then how did the nightwalkers get their—"

The heat that sears me across my face takes my breath away, my cool hands touch my cheek as it feels hot. My eyes glare at her as the burn, distorting my vision of her in front of me. The pressure surrounding my neck increases, and I am lifted from the chair until I can't breathe.

"How dare you compare Breakers to those savages? You will do well not to question what the Great Mother has given us."

She lets go of me, and I feel the chair catch me as I gasp for each breath furiously. I want to inflict the same pain on her as I am feeling. To unleash my pain in any way I can and not care about who is injured. I can't do that, though; I have been down that road, and it only left me with scars that I've hidden well.

I hear the door slam closed behind me, and I let a breath escape my grasp as I stare around the empty room. Moving to the wall, I scan the endless supply of books lined up according to text. History, religion, and war; all that is allowed to be in here. My fingers graze the spines as I search for the one I need.

Reaching upwards, I pull the large book from the top shelf and open it to let a smaller book fall out of it; the Prior and the Wood shines in gold lettering. Considered blasphemy by the Oracle and banned from the palace, Lilliana brought it back with her when she returned from her parents' cottage when we were kids. My fingers caress the red worn leather cover and observe the age that has appeared around its edges.

I flip to my favorite page as I return to my seat. "Each child took their turn with the Prior, lifting their arms in a swooping motion, activating their breaking..." I run my finger across the illustration on the page where the old man, surrounded by the trees, demonstrates Breaking each element for the kids. He taught them how to Break water and collect it for others, tear the ground from itself and use it as shelter, and spark embers from their hands to cook food. As I flip the page, I continue reading aloud.

"Once he had found the children, he taught them the knowledge of Breaking, how to master each element they encountered. After the children finished, he sent them on their way to teach the others. The children taught those around them to Break the elements. Others noticed and wanted the power for themselves; they wanted to control all the elements. The Prior could not let this happen. He spoke to the forest, and defensively it protected him, tangling its gnarled roots so that no intruders may pass." As my fingers cling to the page, my hope for learning to control my Breaking slips and the numbness inside of me shuts everything else out.

"How am I going to save Lilliana?" I whisper as I wrap my arms around myself. The isolation consumes me as I sit with the realization that I am alone; my face touches the coolness of the desk, and the wall stares back at me. I startle when I hear a knock at the door as it swings open loudly.

"Ornae, we have to report to the grand balcony for the public address." Jasmine steps in as she holds the large wooden door open for me.

Chapter 5

Arriving at the grand balcony is easy enough. I take the north wing hallway that leads to the edge of the summer palace. As I approach, I notice the large glass panels that welcome light in, and I feel the heat press into me. My gut tingles as I remember Lilliana and me out on the balcony, watching the snow fall around us like pillows being ripped open and their feathers thrown about. It rarely snowed here in the Summer Palace. We only saw it every couple of cycles. She would always haul me from my bed and drag me out here, shivering as we danced around. My hands cling to my dress, and it brings me back to the present. The intricate charcoal beadwork grates against my fingers and I smooth out the black lace.

Readying myself with a deep breath, we pass through the doorways, and I am instantly confronted with a large crowd staring at us. The mass of people sparkles, clad in all different colors. Some in rich tones of purple and gold stand at the front. I move my gaze to the colorful rainbow that stands in defense of the Nobles. The service guards and Breakers mix among themselves in different color robes, red for HeartBreakers, green for GroundBreakers, blue for WaveBreakers, white for WindBreakers, and orange for BlazeBreakers. My hands still clutch the sides of my dress as I look down at its fabric. Black, the combination of each of the Breakers' represented colors.

"This seems excessive," I say to no one in particular.

Jasmine, at my side, glances at me. "I'm sure they are just trying to make a statement and ensure the safety of the Ornae." She motions for us to sit in the remaining chairs. I move forward out onto the balcony and take my seat next to Commander Kirk; his crimson robe greets me violently in the afternoon sun.

"Yeah, I'm sure," I say, staring out over the crowd of people that have attended today. I imagine the lives they have lived, where they came from, and where they are going when they leave here.

The Marchioness and Marquess take a step forward and wave to the mass of people in attendance. The roar of the crowd is deafening and shouts come from every direction. Unsure where to look or what to do, I just stare forward and smile. Feeling the heat of all the eyes on me.

"Thank you all for coming today," the Marquess booms loudly. A nearby WindBreaker touches his throat to amplify his voice to the crowd, his golden robe flowing down both sides of him in the wind.

"We are sure you have been anxiously awaiting answers regarding the alleged attack on the Summer Palace," he booms.

The crowd stares in anxious silence.

"We want to assure you that you have nothing to worry about. A misunderstanding has taken place with a rebellion. We assure you that this has been taken care of, and thankfully everything is well." His hands raise in warm encouragement, gold glittering out onto the onlookers.

Rage grips my stomach as I stare incredulously at the Marquess, flowing through me as my legs lift me from the chair. I'm halted by Commander Kirk's hand pressing me back down.

"Pick your battles, Ornae," he says lightly. He side-eyes me, and a flat smile takes over his face.

"I can't do this," I say with a shuddered sigh.

"Yes, you can. Just give it a few more minutes, and we can make our way inside." He puts an arm around my chair the way a father may lean protectively over a child. Ever since he trained me to defend myself, he has maintained a stance that the Nobles aren't aware of. Gazing out, I focus on the women in front of us. Large plumes of violet cascade around them as they smile politely at the Marquess.

The Marquess roars louder, "We want everyone to enjoy the upcoming festival and know that everything is still going according to plan. Please enjoy the festivities! May peace from the Great Mother be with you all." He retreats from the dais, his golden robe swaying with his motions, and makes his way back inside with his posse of lower-ranking Nobles.

The crowd erupts in cheers, and horns blow in the distance signaling the beginning of the week-long Moon festival.

"Shit," I say lightly to myself.

I forgot about the Festival of the Moon. It's not like I'm allowed to attend anyway, as it did not fit into the duties of the Voya. From my chamber window, I usually looked out on the far side of the festival, nothing of significance visible except the kids running around the outskirts of the camp getting into trouble or making out behind the game tents.

While I'm lost in thought, Commander Kirk and Jasmine usher us inside from the Grand Balcony, and I feel myself approaching the Marquess without much reservation or thought.

"Why did you tell them nothing happened?" I demand.

"Oh Emma, I'm glad to see you, dear. How are your lessons going?"

"They have a right to know what's going on! So do I!" Staring blankly at his smug face, the age is evident around his eyes, and he offers a weak smile. His silver hair appears disheveled, what's left of it, as it runs to the back of his head like it's trying to get away from his face.

"We don't need to start a panic. The festival brings in a great deal of gold for the kingdom. We know what we are doing," he says eventually.

He's hiding something; I can sense it in my blood. The way it vibrates when I'm next to him. It makes me feel like I'm holding onto a wet snake. My blood continues to boil over, and I feel my fists shaking at my sides. Smoldering with resentment, I turn and nod a forced smile to the other Nobles I notice along the wall. I can feel Jasmine following me as she fixes my dress's train that trails behind me.

"That went well, I think," Jasmine says and looks at me innocently.

"That was bullshit," I choke out.

Chapter 6

After attending lessons with the Oracle, my mind has melted into mush. The history of Nadeem is a long and boring one but something that I am versed in. We covered war strategy today, even though it seems pointless. I won't have to worry about making difficult decisions as Voya since the noble families have each taken responsibility for each sector of the kingdom.

Drifting off in my thoughts, my feet lead me down the west corridor as the bright light shines through the windows. A figure with a sword in a black training uniform catches the corner of my eye. My heart leaps as I approach the window to get a better view.

"Who is that?" I whisper. I move further down the hallway and stopped at a large stone-rimmed window with a full view of the west garden, the figure swings at another figure, flashing a red robe. Commander Kirk lets out an audible grunt, his red robe blowing in the wind as his attacker faces him. I see him take a step back and swing his sword at the assailant, who avoids his swipe and lands behind him, slamming a fist into the back of his head.

Commander Kirk counters and knocks him backward with one blow of his elbow. He leans forward on one hand. If he falls, he isn't getting back up; he taught me that. The dark figure pushes off their back and slides a foot around, catching his feet, knocking Commander Kirk on his back. A gasp escapes me, and the stone sill grinds against my arms as I lean forward out the window. He throws up his hands, and the dark figure's movement slows. He's Heartbreaking him!

I can feel it in them both when he begins, his strength that he's pulsing into his Breaking and the attacker's blood slowing to a crawl. I feel both of their hearts in unison with mine and the blood that runs through our veins. It calls to me as I taste it lingering on my tongue and wanting more.

50

I take off running for the gardens. As I round on the east turret, I lose a shoe coming down the stairs, taking three at a time. As I pass the kitchens, I hear Nora yell something, but I don't stop to catch what she is saying. I open the doors to the east garden and stop in my tracks.

The dark figure approaches, and I slide behind the wall. How did this person stand a chance against Commander Kirk? As the figure comes around the corner, I brace myself and step close. Fear threatens to take root inside me, but I can't cave to it. I spring up behind him and move to take him down, lifting him with my arms. The figure twists as his feet leave the ground and bring me down with him. I lift myself, rolling with the figure, holding each other tightly. "Ornae?" A screech mumbled from behind the mask.

The dark figure releases his grasp as he pulls off his mask and reveals that he isn't a man at all, but rather a woman with the familiar reddish-brown skin tone that I have seen in my chambers helping me get dressed.

"Jasmine?!" I yell. "What are you wearing? Why are you and Commander Kirk fighting?"

"It's called training, and we do it regularly. This would be my training uniform."

"You're a lady's maid." I stare at her curiously. I think back to my view from upstairs and how she was able to take him down.

"I'm also a service guard, and it wasn't easy," she replies as she folds the black mask in her pockets and wipes sweat from her stained brows with her sleeve.

"But you are not. You can't Break... can you?"

"No, I can't, which makes me perfect for the job. The Breakers are needed to fight the war with Navak at the border."

"Train me," I interrupt her. Seriousness spreads across my face.

"It seems someone already has with the way you grabbed me," she replies.

"Not well enough, I'm afraid."

Commander Kirk appears beside us and looks at me sternly. He lifts us off the ground as we dust ourselves off.

"Teach me how to combine my Breaking with combat." I look to them both.

"I've risked my neck to teach you how to defend yourself. Your Breaking isn't reliable." He raises his voice as we have had this conversation, ever since he stopped training me in combat.

The bottled-up rage I held is released. "I have to learn! Those dirtbags in navy uniforms took Lilliana, and I seem to be the only one who cares!"

He stares at me for a moment before answering, "Well, you're not. We've sent a team to retrieve her."

I freeze at his words. "Have they found her?"

"She has not been located as of the last update from the search party."

"Well, then that's not enough! Send another team, send everyone!" I say to his back as he begins to walk away.

"I'm not having this conversation with you anymore. I shouldn't even have shared this with you." He throws up his hands as he marches back inside the palace through the large ornate stone archway.

Now it's just Jasmine and me as we both stare at the empty path in front of us. I look to her. "I have to save my friend," I say pleadingly.

"I'm not even a Breaker," she replies defensively, raising her arms in defeat. "How are you going to save her?"

"You can teach me. Once I control the elements, no one will stop me." I feel the fierceness take me over, and I stare directly into her eyes. They are like amber, reflecting gold in the sunlight.

"What happens if they find out?" She motions her head towards the palace; she means the Nobles.

"Then we are both punished, you banished and me, locked away again." She clicks her tongue as the awkward silence lengthens. "If it means saving Lilliana, then I'll take whatever punishment they have for me, and I'll vouch that you knew nothing."

Jasmine stares at me curiously and lets out a deep breath. "Show me your Breaking." She starts walking towards the back of the garden, gravel crunching under her boots. "Let's see what you can do."

The water from the small creek at the back of the garden dribbles over rocks, and the rush hits my ears. Making sure we are not visible from the palace, I take a deep breath and step closer. The dry grass crunches underneath my boots as I move forward and lift my arms. The water listens as I grab ahold of it. Its shiny surface lifts out of its normal flow, separating itself from the rest of the creek, and floats towards me. The afternoon sun reflects in hues of tangerine through the water, and I hear the crackle of dry leaves.

"Fascinating," Jasmine adds flatly. Her abrupt statement takes me by surprise.

Losing focus, the water sways with itself as it flows in front of me, unstable as it rocks. I look at her, and it crashes to the ground and splashes my dress.

"I thought the Ornae was supposed to be able to command waves that submerged entire towns, shatter the ground itself, and level kingdoms," she questions as she moves closer to me, holding her mask and still wearing her black combat uniform.

"They are…We are." I try to draw the water up from the ground, straining to draw it from where it landed. I try to focus as I hear a song coming from across the stream behind me. Turning up my ear, I listen to it and release the water back into the ground.

"Everything okay?" she questions me as the wind swings at her braids.

"Yes. I thought I heard something…" I pause for several moments, still trying to listen to it. It's gone. "I was mistaken."

"Okay, try again. Let's see you lift the water again. I want you to try to shape it this time, then shoot it towards me." She motions a readying stance.

Taking a deep breath, I concentrate and pull it again from the stream. The crystalline liquid lifts and separates from the rest of the turbulent water as it rolls in on itself. It struggles to maintain its spherical shape that I press it into.

"Good, good, now shoot it."

Sweat drips from my brows as I concentrate with every bit of energy that I have. Arms shaking, I press it and let it float towards her as she steps out of the way. Still staring at passing blob in slow motion.

She stares back at me with confusion. "We have a lot of work to do."

Chapter 7

"It was during the great war that the first Voya emerged into ruling. She was powerful and mastered each of the elements. Her first to master was air, summoning gust that would wipe out entire villages. Level homes with one swipe of her arms. She then proceeded to conquer them all, and her Breaking was something to be marveled at." Powerful, but not invincible. "After the ending of the great war, she disappeared, and the noble families searched endlessly for her as they had feared Naluen or Navak had taken her. Revenge for wiping out the soldiers at the border. Nadeem feared another country had taken the Voya and sacrificed her to give the Breakers in their country more power."

"And what did they find, girl?" the Oracle asks me blandly.

"They were not able to find the Voya. She was gone. They suspected that the country of Naluen had taken her or the country to the east, Navak, with whom we still fight to maintain borders today. This led to a new war of the kingdoms, and Nadeem was able to expand its borders."

"Why was that?" she throws back her charcoal robes with frustration.

"Because our Breakers are stronger than those of the other countries. The Great Mother has seen our hearts and blesses us with longevity and strength. The other Breakers are weaker and have difficulty controlling their Breaking." I say in monotone as I turn to face the window.

The Oracle continues to stare at me in silence.

"Do you think the Voya disappeared in the tangled wood?" I interject as I am brought back to the presence of the room.

She sits up out of her chair. "What's your point?"

"It just seems like maybe she didn't want to be found."

Maybe she ran away to be with the Prior, I think but don't say.

I think back to the children's storybook, where the gnarled

roots of the trees wrap defensively across the page. Others had

wanted his power, and he would not let them have it. "For

someone so powerful, maybe she was protecting herself."

She is across the room before I can register that she

even moved from her chair at the front of the room. "What are

you suggesting? That her own court would somehow betray

her?" Treason, I think, is not a light accusation. Her dry, scaly

skin and grey fingernails wrap around my neck and squeeze

tightly.

"No." Rage boils inside of me as I stare defiantly back

at her.

To my left, I see Jasmine moving off the wall where the

books are stored and placing her hand around her back. I stare

up into the Oracle's sunken eyes and see her slicked-back gray

hair shining in the little light through her hood.

"Then continue" she releases my neck, and I swallow the bile and hatred that threatens to come out.

"I'm just not sure the Great Mother—" I stop when she turns quickly, raising a hand to give me a slap, and I ready myself for the crack against my right cheek.

When the slap doesn't arrive, I open back my eyes and see Jasmine holding the Oracle's left arm in a tight grip.

"How d-d-dare you—" she stutters in shock.

"You will not harm the Ornae."

The Oracle begins shaking Jasmine off as she steps back. I stare in shock as the Oracle registers the situation for a moment and takes a step back.

"You are going to regret that move, girl." The Oracle points a long-crooked finger at her.

Jasmine smiles brusquely and retorts, "We will see about that, I swore to protect and serve the Ornae, and that means from everyone, including you."

I have never seen rage burning in the Oracle's eyes like this before. She stares silently at Jasmine for a quick second and then storms out of the room, slamming the large oak doors behind her.

I rub my throat in a massaging circle and look at Jasmine as I hear the door slam shut behind us. "You shouldn't have done that," I mumble to Jasmine as she stares blankly at the door.

"Why, Ornae?" she questions and presses her hand on the desk in front of me. I see her long black lashes that curve around her glowing eyes.

"Because I can take care of myself." I stare back at her as she leans against the stone wall. "Why do you call me that?" I ask.

"Are you not the Ornae?" She lifts my chin to look at my neck and seems pleased that there are no marks.

"Yes, but everyone calls me Emma." I push her hands away from my desk as I gather the books to put them up.

"Maybe I am not everyone. What do you want me to call you?" she questions.

"Emma is fine." Moving to the back of the room, I open the heavy oak doors and look over my shoulder. "We have to get ready for the Moon Ball this week. Are you coming?"

Since the Nobles do not attend the festival with the commoners, they hold their own ball and invite the wealthy merchants here to drink with them. It is mandatory attendance for the Ornae and future Voya, so I will be expected to be present and polite to everyone. Which makes me exhausted just thinking about it. It is comforting to know that Jasmine will also be forced to be in attendance. We can suffer the night together, at least.

My stomach pains for Lilliana as I think of her. She would love to be eating the fancy cheese and drinking ale all night. We would stay up giggling as we talked about the Nobles and who achieved the drunkest stupor.

Once we reach my chambers, Jasmine closes the door behind her as she comes in. I hear the click of the door as my prison envelops me. I won't be allowed to roam since my lessons are over for the day. My bed welcomes me with a cool embrace as I plop backward onto it. Staring up at the ceiling, dust lifts, and I smell the fresh scent of my sheets.

"I just don't understand how you're the future Voya of Nadeem, yet you have no say in anything you do. You're a prisoner in your own kingdom." She continues picking at her nails with her long-serrated knife. I hate that she's right, and she has so delicately reminded me of what I know and have tried to forget.

"Sometimes, I find myself thinking of running away from this place. Finding the Prior and saving Lilliana. I could find her faster than any of those trackers." Tears threaten to erupt as my eyes burn furiously. "Once I learn to control my Breaking, I will be unstoppable."

"Then why don't we?" She smiles as she follows closely behind me.

I roll my eyes at her and detect the sarcasm laced in her words. It pains me as I want to leave so badly; it twists and aches my gut.

"Yeah... right." I feel the disheartening sensation continue to rise as the fear speaks to me. Looking up, I stare at my closed door and feel the heartbeats outside of it. Guards posted along the rooms "to ensure my safety," as the Marchioness had explained. I lay back with the realization, I will never leave this place.

Chapter 8

Early the next morning, I make my way to the window to look out at the festival being set up. I notice the tents being erected with yellow and red stripes that curve from top to bottom. The men pulling the poles with all their strength and yelling at one another not to drop the ropes. I eagerly watch them put the festival together by hand and drift off slowly into a world where I am part of their interactions. Walking around and yelling back at the men to get where they need to be and make sure they don't forget their tasks.

I see the kids trailing behind the tents, scampering around with balloons in one hand and heated candy drops in the other. They scream and giggle as they chase one another around the tents moving back and forth with the laughter that brings a smile to my face without me noticing it. I envy their freedom, their carefree ability to run and play with naïveté and innocence. I feel a pull in my center, a feeling of tightness entering my chest and forcing me to have a seat. After changing from my morning gown, I look down at the black dress I am wearing today, fidgeting with the beadwork that lines the pattern curving my stomach. I wish Lilli were here to help me. She would know what to do.

I make my way down to see Nora and the rest of the kitchen staff to get the daily briefing on what's going on with Nobles when I hear sounds of yelling. My heart races as I make my way to the large oak double doors that lead to the weapons room. I know the service guards and Breakers use this room often for meetings, but it sparks my nerves to think of the GroundBreakers in the garden and the soil-tipped knife that almost became the end of me.

I slide against the large door, wood scratching against my arms as I push up against it, leaning my head on it. I hear the voices getting louder as they come near the door. The door opens, and I spot a green uniform and black plating surrounding Jasmine's crucial parts as she engages loudly with some poor WindBreakers. They seem to be losing whatever argument they are having. After another moment of hiding behind the door, they press on in the opposite direction. Just enough time for me to slip through the doorway and into the weapons room.

As I scan the empty room, I notice the training mats and the large weapons mounted against the walls. The smell of sweat and musk runs throughout the room and threatens my nose as it embraces me. I stare longingly at myself in the far wall mirrors as I see myself leaping onto the mat and making short work of the Breakers surrounding me. Lost in my thoughts, I drift over to the weapons closets that line the wall on the opposite side of the room.

Pulling open the closet closest to me, I look up at the broad swords that hang there. The silver metal gleams back at me, and I pick the first one, eye level with me, and lift it into the air. It's heavy. I swing it forward and feel off-balance due to the weight. My wrist begins to ache as I wield it, and I place the broad sword back onto the rack, and I look at the next closet. I move towards it and open it, the door sounding with a click. More swords line the mahogany racks as I stare up at them in awe.

They are shorter, handles decorated with intricate designs, and blades burning a white silver in the light. I lift the one that catches my eye as it sparkles and I swing it. It feels perfect in my hand. The handle is golden, with lines running around my grip, allowing it to fit well within my grasp. A dagger. I swipe it again in the air, and I feel the heartbeat behind me.

"It seems you've found a toy." I whip around, startled, as I see someone at the door of the training room. I hold the sword outwards and point it, threatening. My hand refuses to lower the dagger. Jasmine stands across the room, leaning against the large double oak doors. Her dark green uniform casts an olive reflection around her, and she smiles at me.

"I was just looking."

She raises her hands in surrender and eyes me curiously. I lower the dagger and tuck it behind the crinoline that surrounds my legs. Its handle still comforting my grip as it points downward. I won't let anyone take this dagger away from me.

"I think you should keep it." She moves from the door and proceeds closer to me. I feel her cool heartbeat as she gets closer, and my own heart races. As she approaches, I notice her braids that shine in the sunlight, glistening coils that wrap into each other and detailed with accents of gold metal. I find beauty in the intricate details of her hair. "I'll inform Commander Kirk that I have checked it out for my personal use."

Quickly I remove the holster from the wooden rack in the closet and attach it to my waist. "I lost my old one. I had found it in the trash that was to be thrown away." My hands shake as I attempt to stick it in the hidden slip of my dress. I fumble with the hole as I place the holster in it.

"Here, let me help." She moves closer and slides the dagger in the holder, then helps slide it in the opening of my dress. I'm careful to pull it out and not destroy my dress in the process.

"Why are you helping me?" The question slips out before I can process, my hand still shaking. If we were caught, the punishment could be death for her. I would be locked up in my chambers again. My only company would be the maid that brought me my meals throughout the day.

"I don't like seeing anyone unable to protect themselves." She stares back at me coolly, and I look up at her in surprise. Her long dark eyelashes catch my attention as they curve outward over her amber eyes.

"Thank you," I squeak out. I turn and press the doors together, sealing them with a click. The shiny wood reflects the light from the room on my face, and I look over at her.

"Do you have lessons today?" She leans against the wall and watches me as I close the doors. I move my dress as it catches, and I start to move towards the door.

"Not today" I'm grateful for my days off from the Oracle, the days where I don't have to worry about making a wrong move or saying the wrong thing.

"Then let's go train in the back garden." She makes her way towards the large tobacco-colored doors, and I hear her boots stomp across the marble floor. Nodding in agreement, I let her lead the way.

Chapter 9

My muscles are burning by the time we finish. It's been two weeks of training, and I still ache all over and have bruises in places that I never thought I would. I lift off the hard rocky soil and stare up at Jasmine, her sleek body covered in a mist of sweat and her muscles curving up her arms like the hills in the mountainside. I look up at her as she lunges over me, swinging her rod. I roll and miss the connection by a hair, then flip backward and land on all fours in a crawl.

It is much easier to move without that stupid dress on. I swing my own rod around. It catches Jasmine at the knee. She buckles, using her rod to guide her; she avoids the ground and flips around on top of me. My back pressing into the ground below us, I stare blankly as I am pinned to the ground. Out of breath, she releases her rod, and I relax again in the dirt.

"You're getting better," she says as she takes my rod with her and places them in the nearby bushes. She moves some leaves and debris over them so that they are not bothered, and we are not suspected of training.

"Thank you, I hadn't noticed," I say while sitting up and rubbing my lower back. I look out around the far edge of the garden and take in the roses. Most of the bushes have been picked for the festival, but some moon roses remain. Their milky white complexion glistens at me as I stare back at them.

"You're fine, just some growing pains is all. You get used to the pain." She plops down on the ground across from me and starts gnawing on some bread and cheese.

"Why didn't you use your Breaking?" she questions as she reaches for her water canteen.

I don't anticipate this question as those around me already know. "Because it's not reliable. My sword is reliable, always there for me." I pat it against the outside of my leg as Jasmine helped me conceal it today in my trousers that she let me borrow. "I feel the vibrations in the elements around me. I can feel the blood rushing through your veins and your heart beating. I can't always Break them, though."

"The Nobles are counting on that." She presses further as she walks over to the chest that she brought in earlier and opens it to pull out a long object wrapped in leather.

"The future Voya has no need to learn to defend herself. She has guards for that," I say mockingly in a tone that resembles the Marquess'. I stare at the indention the dagger leaves around my leg. My heart starts to race as I think of the trouble this could cause me.

Jasmine stares at the rose bushes surrounding us, and I let myself sink into the vibrations around me, losing myself to the song the elements sing.

On our way back into the Summer Palace, I make my way to the kitchens to check on Nora and the kitchen maids. I greet the maids and butlers as I pass them and ask how they are doing. Anna is learning to sew and hem dresses; I know Jake has fancied Anna for some time as he trails behind her and carries the supplies she needs. I head further on down the stairs and am hit with the scent of warm bread and seasonings filling the air. My nose leads the way as I rush into the kitchen and see the operative chaos that is lunch being orchestrated.

"Hello love! Help yourself to the chicken and dumplings on the table there!" Nora calls out over the hustle and bustle that surrounds her. Pots clank together as people whoosh past me with trays heading upstairs for the Nobles.

"What's the occasion?" I move out of the way and lean against a table to let two more people pass with containers of steaming hot substances.

"I'm not sure. I just do as I am told. You know they don't ask for my opinion upstairs. You know I prefer pork myself as well," she says flatly as she continues to put vegetables away on the racks in the corner. Carrots, beets, and potatoes fill the shelves as she commands the others while multitasking with the vegetables.

Making my way over to one of the three islands in the kitchen, I sit on the farther end, out of the way, and carry the bowl Nora pointed towards. I fill a spoon full with the chicken and dumplings and taste it. It's delicious, just like everything else Nora's whips together in this dusty old basement the Nobles call a kitchen. She deserves better. They would never be caught dead down here where the servants tend to the needs of the entire summer palace.

I find it comforting, though, bellied up to the island, watching Nora bark orders and remove pots from the stove and toss them in the sink. What they are or what they need is not for me to know, but I'm amazed at how she navigates the kitchen. I look down at the bricks that make up the floor and the dark brown cupboards with black wrought iron handles. When everyone is out the door and heading upstairs, she makes her way over to me. She smells like chicken and spice as she comes closer, and I see her cheeks are red with exhaustion.

"So, how's the training going with miss Jasmine?" She peels a potato and leans over the counter, winking at me.

"Please don't ever do that again." I hide my face in my arms with embarrassment.

"Well, come on, dear, you have to give me something. I see you two running around this palace together. I can tell she's training you; you're finally bulking up." She pinches my skinny arms and I put down my spoon on the counter and stare down at the dumplings. The pit of my stomach twist as I recall Lilliana and how we used to run around the palace together. Hiding from the Nobles, stealing books, and sneaking off into the bars in the middle of the night.

"I know you miss her, Emma. It's just good to see you happy. I love seeing your smile." She reaches for my hand and presses into it.

"I know. I'm doing this for Lilliana, I will get her back." I smile weakly at Nora and rub my bruised leg as she reaches to wipe the tears from my face. Her hands smell like the vegetables she's been chopping, and I find the scent comforting.

"I've been reading about the Prior, who trained the kids in the Tangled Forest." Hope threatens to spring up inside me as I turn and look out of the kitchen window. "I wonder if he can help me learn to control my Breaking."

I hate the look she gives me. Filled with pity. "Put those fairytales away, dear. If the Oracle finds out you're reading that, it will end up being kindling for my stove sooner than later." She rubs my arm protectively and stares at me.

"I'm not sure they are fairytales, Nora, and she won't find out." I know to be careful with the Oracle. I've learned from my mistakes on how far to push, and I have the scars to prove it. The Prior may be my only shot at getting Lilliana back, and I won't let them take this from me too.

"Well, eat up, dear, you have your lessons soon and then your dress fitting. You know they will want you on full display at the ball."

She pushes away from the counter and tucks tangled hair behind my ear. I know she's right; they plan to parade me around like they always do and act like everything is perfect here. I look back at Nora, who smiles at me with pity as I gulp down the rest of the dumplings and move to place my bowl in the large rinsing tub. I get up to rinse some plates in the large sink and she snatches them away from me.

"Don't worry about that. Just go. I'll handle it." I lean over her and kiss her cheek.

"I don't know what I'd do without you, Nora."

Chapter 10

As I comb my hair, I look out over the moon festival's tents from my window and think of a day when I may attend. The workers are finally finished with the weeks of hard work setting up the tents for tonight; Their arms are black with dirt to the elbows. Many have gone on to complete other jobs as the remaining workers prepare everything for tonight. Kids of the workers run around their feet, playing with one another. I imagine a time when I can taste the fruit on a stick, they serve to them and run with Lilliana to the games. I can feel a heartbeat behind me slowly approaching. When it interrupts my thoughts, I instinctively turn and drop in a swoop to appear behind the figure, pressing them into the window and holding my comb to their throat.

"You're getting better," Jasmine states as she twists to face me. "I'm deathly afraid of combs."

"You would have been easily taken care of had it not been for this poufy dress that I have been fitted in. They need me to be the largest person in the room, apparently." The dress is large, black, of course, and has a bottom to it that would barely fit through the doorway of my chambers.

"Let's go," Jasmine says as she laughs and makes her way to the door.

As we make our way to the Grand Ballroom, I hear the crowd before I see them. We turn the corner on the large marble staircase, and the music starts playing. I look out over the crowd at the mass of bodies in attendance and recognize the colorful robes positioned along the walls. I feel safer knowing the Breakers will be stationed throughout the Ball for protection, but I don't need them. I pat the dagger through the slit of my dress that runs along the length of my thigh.

The high-ranking public members from the village are in attendance as well. They appear to be wearing a clash of colors, reds and greens, oranges, and blues, that swirl together.

I think back to when Nora had tried to explain it to me; each family had a color set that sets them apart from the others. Pressing forward, I make my way down the stairs. Eyes fall over me as I stroll through the crowd. I wish Nora were here. No doubt she is running the kitchen like an army station right about now, making sure these people get fed hot food. Through the crowd, I lose sight of Jasmine, who is no longer by my side, and make my way over to the refreshments when a tug on my arm catches my attention.

"You look lovely tonight, Ornae." I turn to see the Marquess, dressed in the finest gold, his robes hanging loosely over him and glimmering in the candlelight. He's accompanied by some Nobles I have been introduced to before but whose names I can't remember.

"Thank you, your Grace," I say as I try to make an escape, stepping backward.

"How is your new Lady's maid working out?" He catches me before I turn and leans forward. I smell the stench of his breath and look into his dark eyes.

"Very well, I enjoy her company and assistance," I say politely and pull my arm from his grip.

"Not my particular choice, with skin that dark." He takes a sip of his wine, and I hear the giggle from the other Nobles that overhear.

Shock registers in me, heat flashes to my throat. "What does that mean?" I look at him directly.

"Nothing for you to worry about. I know sometimes engagements like these are taxing for the women involved." He reaches to touch my hair as it hangs around my face, and I lean back to avoid his hand. His pink-toned fingers graze by my face, and I see the drunkenness in his eyes. He stares a moment longer than I am comfortable with.

"Is that all, your Grace?" I ask as I begin backing away and turning.

"Yes, yes, enjoy your night, Ornae," he says to my back as I am already making my way to the other side of the room.

The trumpets sound, and our attention is taken to the dais where the Duke and Duchess are positioned. It's rare to see them here in the kingdom, where the Marquess and Marchioness manage everything. Everyone eagerly makes their way closer to get a glimpse of them and hear what they have to say. I stare longer at the Duke; dark hair covers his forehead in a swoop and his beard is neatly trimmed. He is, as always, in his ivory uniform with a khaki cape with gold detailing that reaches the floor. They sure do love their gold, don't they? I think to myself often how they spare no expense when it comes to themselves.

"They almost look like they rule the kingdom." Commander Kirk positions himself next to me amongst the crowd of bodies.

"They do," I say lightly, defeated. They have the power to make the decisions. They control my life and my world until

I am made Voya. I have a hard time grasping that they will transition that power easily.

"You don't believe that," he says, looking intently at me. I'm not sure I do. I'm not sure what to believe, for I can't hear myself think over the fear speaking to me, telling me that I will not escape this life.

"I know," I say, still unsure. Fidgeting with my hands as they hang down in front of me, I lower my head to stare at the beads sewn to the front of my dress.

"Promise me you'll be careful, Em." He never calls me that. I turn to look at him to register the look on his face.

Meeting his gaze, I retort, "I'm always careful."

"Thank you all for coming to the Moon Ball!" the Duke booms out loudly for all to hear, his personal WindBreaker standing beside him with a finger touching his throat. All eyes face the stage, some going so far as leaving flowers by the

Duke in honor of his service. My eyes start to roll back into my head, and Commander Kirk bumps my shoulder with a smile.

"We are glad to start off the festivities with a toast." Everyone raises their glass to the Duke in the direction of the stage, and I find myself accepting a glass from Commander Kirk. We raise them in unison with the rest of the crowd.

"To the Nobles that ensure the safety of our kingdom, the operations of our country, and to the mission of our lives." He raises his glass for the crowd to witness and takes a drink.

"HERE, HERE," the crowd bellows throughout the grand ballroom. I look around to see everyone drinking and cheering the Duke. My eyes roll again, and I get another nudge from Commander Kirk still beside me.

"Eat, Drink, Be Merry, and be sure to enjoy the rest of the week-long festivities!" He exits the dais as the crowd cheers, and the music starts playing again. Commander Kirk grabs my hand as he leads me out into the dance floor.

My feet are killing me in these shoes the maids gave me to wear. The heels sparkle with pearlescent stones that cover them entirely. I slip them off as I put on my worn flats I brought tucked in my dress. As I fit them on, I give the heels to a nearby maid, asking if she will return these to my room, and thank her.

As she leaves, I turn to find Jasmine. As I scan the room, I hear a scream before registering what it is and where it's coming from. It startles me as I search around frantically. The room is in chaos as we hear another screech. I feel a tug on my arm and look to see a crimson red robe situated over top of dark armor, Commander Kirk found me. He moves and positions me behind him, as much as my oversized dress will allow. The room starts to move, the mass of bodies working together like a sea of motion. Whatever it is, I'll be ready for it. I pat the dagger as it sits snugly against my thigh inside the slit of my dress.

We migrate to the back of the room together as we are carried by the crowd. The guards are exploring other areas and making their way towards us. We motion for the exit when we turn, realizing we are heading towards the screaming at the back of the room. It's dark, opposite of the dais where the Duke and Duchess gathered, lined with bins for discarded plates and cutlery. No longer wailing, the lady points at the dark corner opposite the room's exit where decorations were hung.

We had all been facing the other direction and hadn't realized what was going on at the far back corner of the room. Unprepared, I approach the dark unlit area to try and make sense of what I am seeing. I feel Commander Kirk's arms grab me, but I shrug him off. Then it takes me over with horror as I gasp aloud. The crowd murmurs in unison as the realization hits them, and the girl that was screaming runs into the comfort of some Breaker's arms.

It's a body, lying against the back wall, a familiar charcoal robe thrown back, exposing her gray naked body. Has she been here the entire time? How didn't anyone notice this?

Sickness takes over me as I stare, unable to stop, and I feel it

rising like bile in my throat. It's the Oracle. The realization hits

me like a brick to the head. She's dead.

Chapter 11

The Nobles have ordered the service guards to cover the area. Commander Kirk has swept me up and we are now making out way into the main corridor. I search frantically for Jasmine as I jump to look over Commander Kirk's shoulder. I don't see her anywhere. If the killers are still here in the Summer Palace, they could have her, and we wouldn't know. The pained image of the Oracle's body is singed into my eyes for all eternity. Her limp body crumpled on the marble floor like a sack that Nora would put vegetables in to boil. Bile burns as it reaches my throat, and I force it down. Who would want to kill the Oracle? Who could kill the Oracle?

I think to myself that I can't be the only person in the palace that has been mistreated by her. Surprisingly, the numbness that I feel spreads throughout me as I focus on where I am headed.

"Do we know how she died?" I ask Commander Kirk as I try to keep up with him, struggling along the way in my large dress.

"It looked like she was strangled. Maybe choked with something."

I just stare forward as I remember her crusty gray nails poking into my throat each time I questioned her or the history of Nadeem. I rub my neck anxiously as I try to focus on where we are going in the Palace.

I hear the crash of windows and feel the tug of Commander Kirk as I hit the ground, glass raining down on top of us. My arms brace the impact of the cold marble floor beneath us, and my eyes struggle to adjust. I look up to see figures in navy blue uniforms and small gold detailing around the neck and waist. My heart freezes for a second. I know these uniforms, I think to myself, and I leap up, pushing my hands into the broken glass.

Commander Kirk says something to me, but I am not listening. I stand up and unlatch the small dagger from the inside of my dress, tearing the bottom in the process. They took her from me, they tried to kill me, and now they are going to pay. An unknown force drives, giving me strength, as I swing outward, and the dagger swipes through the air furiously. The Naluen soldier isn't ready for my lunge when he throws his hands up, and the floor carves itself to his command, forming on both his arms, solid rock. The crowd explodes, and the soldiers respond instantly. My sword clangs off his rock-covered forearms as they block his chest. I roll instantly to the side, anticipating his swing, and take his feet from underneath him. When he lands on his back, I bring down my sword in his chest and hear the gurgle as it erupts from his mouth. It slices through to the floor like a knife through butter, and I feel myself pulling the sword back out and stabbing him in again and again. I can't stop, and I mutilate his body into pieces.

I feel arms gather around me and pulling me away.

"He's dead. Stop Emma. He's dead." Commander Kirk says as he drags me down the corridor. My feet scrape against the marble stone as they are dragged along with my body.

"There are too many of them. I want you to find Jasmine and return to your chambers." He scans the area and presses forward with me in his grip.

"I'm not going. I can take care of them," I say breathlessly as we round the corner running face-first into Jasmine. She grabs my arms to stop a full-on collision, but our heads still touch.

I rub my forehead. "Where have you been? We have been looking everywhere for you!"

"I have been looking for you as well. We must have gotten separated when the chaos erupted in the ballroom earlier," she explains simply.

"The oracle is dead. Someone killed her. Someone strong," I say breathlessly, leaning my sword against the wall.

"I know." She stares blankly at us both.

"I want you to take the Ornae to her chambers and guard her there. We will send extra guards to assist if we can," he commands Jasmine.

Jasmine nods and attempts to take my arm and lead me away, but I protest and shake her off.

"I'm not going to sit idle in my room while my home is being attacked by these savages. They took everything from me. I will see their blood spilled on these floors." I look up at Commander Kirk and see the stress on his face. His dark eyes, reflecting in the candlelight from the hallway, stare back at me.

"I will carry you if I have to." Jasmine starts to come up to me but is abruptly interrupted by the collapse of the two large doors at the end of the Corridor.

I stare as the navy-blue uniforms fill the hallway on both sides. They smile at us as they fill into the large hallway, and I look to each of them, picking up my sword from the wall. Jasmine pulls her sword from its sheath at her side, and

Commander Kirk raises his hands. I feel the charge of energy shifting off him as it vibrates the blood inside me.

All hell breaks loose. Two men rush the commander, he grips them with both hands straining against the weight of energy his is surging forwards, he makes a swiping motion that I have seen many times. Within seconds both men stop and stare forward in shock until they drop to the ground. Blood begins pooling from their faces like a stream of crimson. It takes so much out of him I can see it in his eyes. He leans forward in time for Jasmine to hop off his back and bring her sword down on another approaching soldier.

I'm frozen in awe as I witness her grace as she leaps from one attacker to another, stabbing along the way. She's so fast I can't register what move she will make until she has already made it. Silence surrounds her as I don't hear her footsteps, just the screams from the men she takes down. She topples the next guy as she brings her foot around to his stomach and connects with a sickening crack. I start to question why they are not breaking; none of the soldiers are competition for her. Another one drops to the ground as she turns in a flash to wipe her sword across another's neck and proceed to push through the gang of men.

"She's strong… and fast," I say to myself as I watch her out of the side of my eyes. I lift my dagger again and thrust it upwards as one of the soldiers rushes me. I'm prepared. I twist and pull, throwing the man to the side.

Commander Kirk positions himself off the ground. "You have no idea." He swipes his sword through the air, and it lands in someone's chest. He reaches out with his hands at two more men.

"Some of them are nightwalkers, be sure to cut off their heads!" she commands to the service guards as they surround the last of the men.

I turn towards her as two more bodies drop beneath her and gulp, "Their heads?"

"Yes, that's the only way to kill them."

I looked around to see the bodies littering the hallway as I leaned against the wall, gazing around me and catching my breath. I place my dagger back in its holster and put it in the slit of my dress. As more guards fill in the large corridor Commander Kirk and Jasmine bark orders and move over towards me.

"I have to provide a report for the Duke and Marquess. Please escort the Ornae back to her chambers for the evening." Jasmine nods in agreement, and I stay silent. We both exit the hallway and silently stroll through the corridors. More guards rush past us on their way to take over for Commander Kirk. I lead the way as we turn left and head downstairs and notice that Jasmine is not following me.

"Your room is upstairs," her arms are crossed, folding her blood-covered green uniform as she stares down at me.

"I know that. I have to check on something else."

Hopefully, she won't ask too many questions. I can't reveal my hiding spot, it's too valuable, and I can't risk not getting information from it.

"You're going to spy on the meeting." My stomach churns as ice creeps inside and threatens to stop my breathing.

I swallow lightly. "How did you know?"

"I know exactly where all of you hiding places are. It's my job." Her smug smile flashes across her face with pride, but then she meets my eyes, and it drops to seriousness. She moves closer as she steps down the stairs and looks directly at me.

"And you haven't reported me."

"No, I haven't. It seems like it's important to you." Her stare eats at me, making me want to look away. Anywhere but directly at her, where her eyes can see through to me.

I interrupt my thoughts and break my eyes away from hers. "I have to find out what's going on." I take a few more steps down hesitantly, wondering if she is going to stop me or if I should make a run for it now.

"Let's go then." She motions towards the end of the staircase, and I take them two at a time. My flats scrape against the stone steps as I glide down them. We press forward, making our way towards the door and cling to the shadows, navigating the halls silently. As we round the corner, I see the small door opposite Commander Kirk's meeting room. I reach for the door, and we enter it silently; I hear the voices on the other side of the room. The cobwebs cling to us as we reach down for the grate and pull ourselves under the table.

"This is disgusting," Jasmine tries to fling the cobweb from her braids as they collect the dust around us. I ignore her as I focus on the figures standing around the room, looking around, trying to identify each person as they speak. They are seated at the large wooden table that sits in the center of the room. The red walls with gold accents reflect the candlelight as it hits the ladies' dresses as they sit around the table.

Commander Kirk is the first to speak as he stands at the head of the table, ferocity spreading across his face. "We have apprehended the intruders. The ones still alive are being held within the lower dungeon."

"Do we know what their intent was this time?" the Duke speaks loudly, casting his voice across the room.

"We believe it was to send a message. The same one they sent with our troops. We have gotten word from the Breakers we sent to retrieve the people they had stolen from us."

Lilliana... My heart aches and it stirs my stomach as I listen.

"What did they confirm?" The Marquess' voice is recognizable, and my eyes roll to him instinctively. He usually has nothing significant to contribute other than telling me what I can't do.

"It was confirmed that their attempt was unsuccessful. The heads of the men were placed on spikes on the edge of the

Tangled Forest." Silence overtook the room as Commander Kirk continued with his report. "We are unsure if we should send another group to retrieve them. It's clear what they wanted tonight. We cannot let them get close to the Ornae." His head hangs as he clenches the papers tightly, his knuckles turning white.

They want me dead! My heart thumps louder in my ears as I struggle to listen further to the group.

"The Naluen soldiers we were able to capture were forthcoming with information. I assume the ones we captured tonight will speak as well." His knuckles crack as he flexes his fist open and closes his grip tightly.

"Then we will have to protect the Ornae. For her own safety, we should seclude her to the higher quarters." The Marchioness' gold dress shines bright in the light from the windows, radiating around her like a beacon.

"No..." I mouth silently to myself. My heart threatens to sink. I grab Jasmine's hand beside me as she looks at me. I silently slide myself out from under the table and sit up from the stone-cold floor. "If I'm not free, then I can't save Lilliana. They are doing nothing to help her, and I won't be a prisoner in my own castle. I'm leaving!"

Chapter 12

While we make our way back to my room, I scrape my nail along the groove in the wall. I think back to the guard I killed tonight and how my sword repeatedly sliced through his chest. It felt good to release the pain, to make him hurt the way I had when they took Lilli from me. I stare down at my shaking hands. My body feels like it's vibrating, and my stomach is in knots. I reach over to grab Jasmine's arm. "Are you coming with me?"

"You've lost your mind." She turns around and heads towards me from the bathroom. "I hope you know that."

"If they aren't going to protect me, then I have to find a way to protect myself. I'm going to find the Prior." I continue packing my bags with necessities that I think I will need.

"You're going to go off chasing fairytales when we were just attacked by people that literally want you dead." She steps in front of me as I attempt to make my way to my room.

"They want me dead whether I stay or not."

"I still don't like the idea," she says as she crosses her arms.

"You're welcome to come along if you wish. Just stay out of my way." I give her a look of seriousness that I haven't before.

"Oh yeah, that's a great idea. I let you run off while I stay and get thrown in the pits by the Duke and Marquess." The sarcasm in her voice becoming much too apparent.

I enter my room and fish for my things, the stale aroma fills me, and I try not to let it get to me. I fish for the book; its red leather-bound spine feels familiar under my touch, and I put it in my bag. After I finish getting dressed, I show Jasmine what I have been working on collecting.

"A maid's uniform?"

"They will recognize me if I wear the black dresses." I toss them back onto the bed with the rest of them in exchange for the uniform.

"They will recognize you. Period," she retorts as she leans back against the wall in her dark plated uniform. "Are you really ready for this?"

"I am," I say as I lift my bag over my shoulder. I'm tired of not having a say. I'm tired of being a prisoner in my own kingdom.

"Alright then," she resigns and steps out of my way. "How are we going to do this?"

"I have already thought of that. Grab everything you want to take with you." Heat flashes towards my neck as I think of the exit Liliana and I have used so many times. How we would giggle as we run out into the night with our robes billowing in the wind as we made our way to the pubs.

"I'm already ready. Just say when and where." She smiles at me.

106

"Great, let's go to the kitchens."

As we approach the kitchens, solemn silence fills the air, the sound of chairs scooting and clinking silverware comes from the servants' dining room. They must be having their dinner, finally, after everyone else has eaten. I navigate the hallways with ease as this is my favorite place in the palace. I find comfort in the smell of homely hallways. We reach the room and peek inside to witness everyone at the long dining room table. Its large wooden boards collect unevenly as it seats twenty people. I scan the room and notice the furniture is mismatched with some chairs from sets, which are broken. As we press forward, we reach the end of the hallway where the pantry is located. The root vegetables and grain are stored in here. We make our way into the room as the smell of dirt hits us overwhelmingly. My eyes water as I reach out for the robes hung on the opposite wall. The darkness doesn't allow for much to be seen as I stumble through crates and baskets of potatoes.

"Going somewhere, dear?" It's Nora, her familiar voice echoes throughout the pantry.

"I'm leaving," I turn and say to her quietly.

"What's going on?" She rubs my arms that are tucked around me.

"I'm going to find the Prior and save Lilliana. I can't stay. They will lock me up," I announce proudly to her.

She stares at me and looks over to Jasmine, and then back at me. "How are you going to find them, dear?"

"The book says he was in the Tangled Forest, where he taught the kids to use their breaking and control the elements. So that's where I am going to start." I open my bag slightly for her to see the supplies and books that I have gathered.

"Great idea, right Nora?" Jasmine

She's silent for several seconds and then looks at me.

"Yes," Nora says, ignoring Jasmine and staring at Emma. "If

you really want to do this, then you have my support dear." Nora stares directly at Jasmine. "And if anything happens to her, a pig won't be the only thing I roast," she threatens.

Jasmine raises her arms in retreat as Nora leads the way further through the pantry to the back door covered by shelves of preserved jams.

"You're not going on an empty stomach, I know that. Take some of these with you, they won't be missed." She reaches to the shelves and pulls jars of jam, blocks of cheese, and some bread into a bag.

Nodding, I look over at Nora, still in her apron, stains running along the front where she whipped together tonight's food.

"I will be back, I promise," I say, bringing tears to my eyes in the process.

She wraps her arms around me and squeezes tightly. "I know you will," she says smiling back at me through her tears, and she leaves the pantry, closing the door behind her.

I wipe my eyes on my sleeve as the tears fall down my cheeks and we press forward. Making my way from the servant's entrance to the stables. I know many of the stable hands will be in bed by now. They will have to be up to feed in the morning. As I get closer, the smell of manure hits me, and I see the horses lined up, the moonlight casting itself on each of their faces as they sniff us. Their dark hair glistens. I count the horses, nine in total on this side of the stable. They won't miss one then.

"Can you ride?" I ask, looking at her.

"Yes, can you?"

"No. I was never taught." I admit. They would never have provided me with the means or skills to escape.

"Ride with me then. Let's take the big one." She points towards the large horse; its towering frame stands several feet above me. As we approach, it nuzzles my hair searching for treats. She saddles the horse with the one hanging from the wall and straps it's in. I place my bags on each side, and my back is grateful for the release.

"Ready?" She questions, looking over her shoulder at me.

I nod silently in approval and look back at the summer palace as we gallop towards the Tangled Forest.

Chapter 13

We migrate closer to the forest. We cannot afford to stop. Once the Nobles leave Commander Kirk's meeting, they will be looking to move me to the lower quarters. I will be contained and never meet the prior or set Lilliana free.

"My bum is killing me," I protest as I rub my lower back.

"You'll get used to it. I used to ride with my dad as a kid. We would ride for days at a time. I love it." A tone lays in her voice, and I struggle to see her face as my view is the back of her head. Sorrow mixed with a hint of anger, it's new to me as I listen closer and feel her tension.

"I wish I could share your experience." I readjust myself on the saddle as my bum has already gone numb and is tingling. Hoping that she continues to share more of her story.

"So where are we going? Once we are in the forest?"

"I'm not sure. The book says the Prior will find those that need him most." I pull the book out of my bag and thumb the worn red leather; its gold lettering glints softly in the moonlight.

"I know... Emma, I just keep wondering if the Prior is even real," she questions and looks out into the night sky. The lights of the summer palace have grown to tiny dots in the distance as I search for them.

"I know, I was thinking the same thing. I believe he is, though." I lean forward to show her my book that I keep close by, and she takes it hesitantly, still holding the reins in her other hand.

She flips through the pages, intrigued by the pictures. "It's too dark to read now. I can barely make it out. I do think being closer to nature will definitely help you with your Breaking."

"It's worth a shot, though, right?" I ask, more for myself than for her.

"We will see," she replies weakly and hands me back the book. I tuck it back in my bag and flip the flap over top, securing the latch.

As we reach the edge of the forest, I look across the endless spread of trees lining the front. I reach for her hand as she helps me down from the saddle, and I plop my legs on the ground, still numb from the uncomfortable ride. I ignore her comments as I turn to stare at the Tangled Forest, perfectly aligned with the edge of the grass.

"We are going in there?" I ask. I look around and notice a wagon to our side. Its busted wood glints softly from the lantern that hangs from a hook on the back. I inspect the broken down one-wheeled disaster and realize the wood is cracked and split in half as I get close.

"What do you think did this?" I ask as I run my finger over the shattered pieces surrounding the wagon.

"No idea." She says brightly as she takes the lantern from the back of the wagon. "They won't be needing this, I assume."

As I turn, we lead the horse with us down to the entrance of the trees, gnarled together with gray bark that darkens behind the moon. The path at my feet fades as I find myself entering the darkness of the woods. Somewhere in this mother-forsaken place are the answers I need. My small flat feet tread the naked dirt as I pass roots and leaves.

Further in the wood, we navigate the path not by sight yet by faith. After several hours of walking, I notice the pain starting up my right ankle. My feet are killing me, I think to myself. We help the horse navigate the terrain carefully as it lowers its head to duck between branches. Jasmine trots along in front of us and presses further into the brush, hacking away with her sword as vines and bushes try to consume us.

"We can stop and make a fire," she says as she reaches for her own bag she brought with her. "I brought provisions and stole some food from the kitchens before we left. The horse will need some water too."

"You didn't have to steal it. Nora would give you anything you asked for, she gave us food as well," I say, wary of what she will pull out. I pet the horse's face as it nuzzles my pockets and pulls on my dress with its teeth.

"She didn't need to know. We can't afford to bring others down with us." Jasmine examines the area and moves around, listening to the wind.

She's right. I stare at her under the moonlight. Her ebony skin mingled with the blue light is magnificent. Her hair is braided back in long braids that twist from top to bottom, where they are clasped by gold metal detailing. The shadows carve out her muscles on her lean body and pronounce her breasts. This realization hits me as I notice her body, fully, for the first time. She's beautiful, I think to myself.

"If you keep staring at me like that, we may have a problem." She winks at me as I realize I am facing her.

116

Blushing, I reply, "I wasn't staring. It's just hard to see what you're doing in this light."

She strikes the flint on the kindling and blows lightly. I can feel the embers working to ignite. I feel the vibrations on my skin as soon as they catch. Smoke trails up to her face as she waves her hand trying to dissipate it from the air in front of her.

"How did you learn to do that?" I say as I realize how little I know of her.

"My dad taught me. He taught me a lot of things." She continues to work with the embers, and they shoot into the sky. I hear a plop that rattles the forest ground below us as I see the horse has laid down.

"Really? What's he like?" I search for a flat grassy piece of ground to lay out the blankets for us to sit on.

"He's a tough man, firm, but kind."

"Do you get to see him or your mother often?"

"My mother didn't survive my birth. My dad, I see sometimes, he has a complicated job though."

"I'm sorry." I look down at the blanket she has laid out and plop myself down on it.

"It's okay, I've learned to accept my past for what it is. It's what brought me here." She smiles at me. It's contagious, and I smile back at her. It feels good to be out of the palace. I've never been this far from it and it's exciting yet terrifying at the same time.

I move over to sit closer to her on our blanket. "I never knew my parents. I was found abandoned by Nora, who found me on her way to the Palace and brought me with her. She fed me while working and then reported me to the Nobles. She continued to care for me until I was five, that's when everyone is tested, and it turned that I was the one they were all looking for."

"The Ornae, the future Voya, found by the kitchen staff abandoned as an orphan." She jabs her elbow at me jokingly.

"Yeah yeah, write it down and sell it." I retort back to her.

"We should get some rest," Jasmine says as she lays down on her back on the blanket. I lay down next to her, staring up at the sliver of stars visible through the branches of the trees. The night is peaceful, a slight breeze, just enough to feel cool. I hear the insects in the distance and listen to what they have to say. I come back to the present and feel the warmth and vibrations from the fire, reminding me that it's there.

"It's beautiful, isn't it?" I say aloud. After a moment of no response, I lean up to look at her. Her chest rising and falling with a soft breath releasing from her. I lay back down and gaze up at the sky above me, marveling at its beauty. Sometime later, I drift away.

SQUAKKKKK!

"What is that?" I rise up, yelling. My heart races as I look around frantically, remembering where we are and how we got here. Rays of sunlight drift through the verdurous canopy surrounding us. They penetrate through the leaves and cast a green-gold luminescent coat across the ground. I stare up into it as my eyes adjust and recognize the varying shades of green flatly panned leaves that brushed around us as we slept.

Jasmine is already up; she grabs for her knives and pours water on the smolders from last night. Where did she get water? "I am not sure what it is, but it seems to be coming from above us. We better get moving soon," she states as she scans the clearing, looking up at the sky.

"Great," I say as I get up and stretch. Sleeping on the ground is not what I had envisioned for a good night's sleep, and I feel it in my back. I look around for my sword and realize it's on the other side of the blanket. It's then that I see something shiny out of the corner of my eye, on the other side of the clearing. Moving that way, I pass by Jasmine, who is packing up the blankets and discarding the pile of burning wood.

"Best if nobody notices we were here," she mutters to herself, kicking dirt onto the fire.

I keep moving to that side of the clearing and feel myself pulled in a certain direction. My center is being pulled by a rope that constricts my body and doesn't want to let me go. Telling me that I need to follow it or else I may rip apart.

"Emma? Em?" Jasmine tries to call for me.

I keep walking across the grass, following the sweet song that fills me until I hear a THOOM land behind me. Distracted, I come back to the present surrounding me, losing the grip of the invisible force that was pulling me towards it. Before I turn, I notice the large shadow cast above me; I turn to see the largest bird I have ever seen. Its feathers are coated in hues of purples and orange, and a black beak that protrudes from its face above me. As I stare up in awe at the magnificent creature, I look down to notice its razor-sharp claws dug into the soil.

"EMMA! DO NOT MOVE!" I hear Jasmine call across the clearing as she dashes towards us.

The bird looks closely at me, and with its large beak, it lets out a roar that would strike fear in the Commander himself.

Naturally, I run. My feet lead me away from the giant bird.

I fear this giant creature will rip the meat clean from my bones in one bite, and it will still not be satisfied. As I run, I hear a flap of wings and feel the gust of wind hit my back, knocking me to the ground. I bite into the dirt and roll over on my back, staring upwards. I pat my thigh as I reach for my dagger, and my stomach drops. It's still on the blanket!

Terror deciding my every move, I scream loudly and feel the vibrations of the ground below me singing back to me and pouring into me like water flowing into an empty vessel. I call to it and allow it to engulf my body with the energy I didn't realize I needed. Tiny spots of dirt and sand start to envelop me, with grass tugging at my body, casting itself across my arms and legs. The bird's razor-sharp beak lunges for me, and grass fills its jaws, gagging the bird. I let myself sink deeper and realize I am stuck within the ground that has cocooned me, covering my head. I feel the impact of the beak as it strikes and rips at the grass and soil. It reacts to my fear and command, continuing to wrap itself thicker.

I hear a slash and a thud as something large hits the ground and the beak disappears. I'm blind to the world in this cocoon and soon hear Jasmine's voice, "Emma, are you in there? What did you do?"

"I'm not sure. I don't know what happened." She begins ripping at the grass, trying to help me get out, but it keeps growing back. Reaching out to me as if it longs for my touch. I feel tense with anxiety as it keeps sprouting, and I wonder if I am going to die in here. Then I feel my chest relax and my center fully decompress, the grass retreating.

"I think I need to relax, and it will let me go." Jasmine is still trying desperately to pull at the grass and dirt. I take a deep breath and feel myself let go, the energy flowing from me to the ground. I say a silent 'thank you' to it as it pushes me up and releases me. The earth retreats, and I'm left lying on my back, staring up at the clouds. I let Jasmine lift me up off the ground, and when I look at her, I wrap my arms around her torso and squeeze tightly.

"Thank you," I say breathlessly.

She stares at me, pausing slightly as she then leans forward and hugs me back. Just long enough so that I could inhale her scent, feel the warmth of her skin pressed against mine. The touch of her was everything I needed as I felt her arms coming around my back and pulling me forward. I pull away from her, smiling, and look to my left at the ground.

"I'm glad you're okay."

"Did you have to cut its head off?" I ask, looking to my left at the giant purple and orange chicken.

"That's how you kill things, remember?" She smiles smugly at me. Lowering her blood-covered sword as she wipes it off with a bunch of orange feathers.

"Yeah, I know. I'm not sure what happened, though." Rubbing my arms at my sides. "The ground trapped me." It wouldn't let go of me.

"I think it protected you..." She gestures to the clearing surrounding us.

"What do you mean?"

"I think you Broke the ground. You're a GroundBreaker, Em."

Chapter 14

Making our way through the humid summer forest, I
notice the bugs zipping around me as we continue deeper. We
don't see much of a path, but we continue making our own
way, Jasmine, using her sword to hack through the bushes. The
bugs scurry out of sight and hide beneath bristles of wispy
moss. Walking in and out of the shady glades, the smell of the
air is enticing and smells like the garden of the Summer Palace
right before it rains.

"How do you know where to go?" I ask skeptically. "I
can't even tell where we are. It all looks the same."

"I'm not sure. There has to be something out here in
this stupid forest."

"I don't think it appreciates being called names," I chide as the vines lean towards me while I walk. I let them caress me as they provide a loving touch of comfort.

"You're enjoying this, aren't you," she snarks as she hacks through to pave the way for us. Sweat starts to bead at the nape of her neck, and I stare as it glistens off her. She turns to stare at me, staring at her, and I look longingly at her long black eyelashes.

"I feel alive, Jasmine. I feel for once that I am free. I've never felt this before. I used my Breaking to defend myself. I've never been able to do that!" We march on, and I gaze up at the trees and breath the air deeply, letting my shoulders sag with an exaggerated exhale.

"Uh-huh, amazing. We should see if we can find the Prior soon. If not, we may have to turn back." She motions for me to follow her, and we continue.

We come up to a worn dirt path that forks as it hits a flatline of dense trees.

"He should be finding us. Which way should we go?" I question, standing on my toes to see down both paths. I feel the song pulling me in the direction to go right. That same pull that called me across the clearing and led me to my near death.

"Left, we have to go left." She looks at me with fierceness in her eyes and starts making her way down the left path. I run after her and question, "Why this way?"

"Because it's the path we should take, Em. Trust me." She glares at me with seriousness, and I lift my arms in defeat.

I do trust her. I've trusted her with my life, which explains why I am here right now with her on this path in the middle of the Tangled Forest. I look over my shoulder longingly in the other direction and feel the distance being placed between us. Like two magnets being pulled apart and fighting to reconnect.

"Okay," I say as I connect with her hand and skip along the path. She smiles at me and squeezes my hand tighter.

We move forward and press ourselves uphill as the path demands, and when we reach the top, it's all I can do to plop down on the ground. Breathing deeply, covered in sweat and dirt from the journey here. I lay back, feeling the ground pressing into me as I stare up at the sky. It's more visible here at the top of the hill and less covered in trees. I roll over onto my stomach and feel the world turn to witness the beauty of the forest. Lush evergreens as far the eye could see, sprawling points that rustle in the wind, it sings to me calling it, wanting to lift me up and carry me. I breathe deeply and exhale, blowing the grass below my chin back and reveling in how alive I feel.

Catching her breath as well, Jasmine is hunched over, nibbling on bread and cheese she stole from the kitchens. "Do you want some?" She motions the pieces towards me.

"No, thank you," I politely decline as I continue to stare out at the horizon.

"I don't see how you're not hungry." She consumes the rest of the bread and places the cheese back in her big bag.

"I just don't feel hungry here. I feel alive." Reaching my hands up into the air as I attempt to grab the stars themselves. I let myself roll around on the ground. I think to myself, that's the only way to describe it. I feel as though, for the first time, I can breathe. That if I leave the ground, I may never come back down again.

Jasmine stares like me as if I have gone mad, and let's go a small laugh. "We better keep moving. We don't want another run-in with a Warrot." She gets up off the rock she was sitting on and packs her bags. Slinging them over her shoulder. I notice for the first time her hair is coming unbraided.

"Your hair," I say, reaching out to touch the folded strands of black hair. "It's coming undone."

"Yeah, it was bound to happen. That's what I get for sleeping on the ground."

"I wish I knew how to braid; I would fix It for you."
Letting go of her hair, I breathe her in, her smell, like that of
rose petals dipped in honey.

"It's fine, I'll have to have it braided eventually, but I
may just let it down soon." She motions for us to continue
forward, and I press on. Carrying my bag on my back and a
stick I found in my right hand, we make our way down the
slope.

On our way down the hill, I continue to stare up to the
sky and stretching out my arms to feel the tree branches as they
pass. They want to hold me, keep me here with them, and I am
willing to let them as they pet me. I reach out to them from
inside and feel the vibrations singing to me, the entire forest
fills me, and I let go of a gasp as I release it.

"You need to pay attention, Em. I don't want us to go
sliding down this." She seems concerned, so I try to steady
myself as we make our way downwards. The hill is steep, and
my flat shoes are more fit for the summer palace hallways than

the rocky terrain of this hill. Before Jasmine notices, I feel my feet slip out from underneath me as I roll down the hill. Rocks attempt to stop my tumble as they jab into my side. I hear a sickening crack as a log halts my body to a stop.

Above me, I hear Jasmine calling out my name and her arms around me. I attempt to orient myself and tell her that I am okay, even though I do not feel okay. The pain comes like lightning across my side as I take a deep breath.

"Em, can you hear me?" She shakes me until I feel my brain rattle inside my head.

"I'm fine," I cough as she sits me up and holds her hands around my face.

I attempt to brush her off, but her assistance is comforting. The forest is much different from the Summer Palace. The guilt sits in that I may have made an impulsive decision to make this trip. I feel childish, and the heat comes on strong to my chest and neck. I will not cry, I tell myself. I rub my side where the log hit me. I may have a broken rib, I think to myself as I inhale shakily.

The husky voice that I hear next comes from the corner behind us, "It seems you two got lost." Before I can turn around to see who else is in the forest with us, I see Jasmine's eyes dart back and forth, readying her sword, the ground consumes us.

Chapter 15

I come to as I orient myself to my surroundings, staring

up, my head tilted towards the sky. I smell the forest around me

as crisp pine flows into my nostrils. Dazed, I attempt to sit up

and am unable to move my body. Fear spikes inside me as I

attempt to writhe frantically and focus on my surroundings. I

gaze down at my body and see the ground staring back at me,

reaching towards my neck. Have I sunken into the ground? No,

a frightening realization hits me, it has raised up to engulf me,

covering me entirely up to my neck. I feel the pressure of the

compact terrain sealing around me as I attempt to move. It

won't budge. I realize this as I force my limbs harder against

the walls of the dirt. They scream in pain as I bite down. I

attempt to connect with the landscape, begging it to let me go.

It whispers to me, but it won't Break. I let out a sob as I look

around for Jasmine to make sure that she is safe.

"Ah, you're awake. About time." The man approaches in a navy uniform outlined with gold detailing, except he has more gold than the others. Naluen Solider, I think to myself. No, Naluen Commander? I question acknowledging the differences between his uniform and those of the other officers approaching. The others face my way with their arms stretched out. I feel the ground Breaking to their will. They are why it won't listen to me; I am no match for even one of them.

"Why are you doing this?" I question him as he smiles slightly. "What have you done with Jasmine?" I scream.

"Don't worry, your little bodyguard is safe." He stands across the forest of discarded debris and stares, a smug look on his face.

"How did you find us?" I question, looking around at the others approaching us.

"Oh, I thought you were smarter than that." He clicks his tongue at me, shaking his head. "And here she comes now."

Before I can register what he is saying, I see Jasmine

walking forward, her head hanging low, as she approaches the

Commander and shakes his hand. Fury erupts within me as I

comprehend what I am seeing. They talk for some time, and I

hear their words and see what is happening in front of me, but

it is like my brain can't process any of it. Tears immediately

come streaking down my face, and I grit my teeth together. My

brain processes it further, but my heart denies it, not allowing

the full realization to surface.

"We should talk." Jasmine turns towards me.

"Talk?" A laugh escapes me, and it sounds wrong.

"I'm sure you have a lot of questions."

"DON'T!"

The next breath I take burns my throat. Oh, Great

Mother, I know what is going on here. My head buzzes as I

glare forward at her, arms folded across her slim chest.

"Why! Why would you do this?" I scream at her as she

stands next to the Naluen Commander and looks at me,

deadpan. I swallow a dry rasp as it escapes, and I feel the fire burn my lungs. It grows inside my center as it becomes white-hot. I stare directly into her eyes. My passion sparks instantly, sizzled out by the inferno that rages in my heart. It is all I can manage to lift my head and glare at her. She drops her head and avoids my gaze.

"I trusted you! I..." my voice trembles as I speak. I flail wildly, attempting to get free from the ground and fight her. I want her to hurt like she has hurt me. I want her to feel that pain that I feel.

"Awe, she's grown attached to you," the Naluen commander retorts as he smacks Jasmine on the back and pushes past him.

"We were supposed to meet you all going the other direction at the fork in the path, but it seems someone got lost." He stares pointedly at Jasmine, who is still staring forward at the ground, "Good thing we avoided those Nadeem trackers and met you all here," he exclaims as he approaches me, still trapped in the raised soil with grass up my neck.

"Leave her alone, Gavin." Jasmine reaches for his shoulder, and he stops walking towards me. "You said we would capture her and bring her back to Naluen with us. Let's finish the job."

"Yes, let's," he replies to her while he stares at me. "You wonder why we did this. You will soon understand. Or should I let your dear Jasmine tell you?" He motions towards her and places his arm around her neck, leaning on her.

"Why don't you tell her how you began to earn her trust?" He snorts a laugh as she pushes him off.

At first, I feel like I've been dipped in an ice bath, then my cheeks burn hot with fury, and a guttural cry leaves my mouth as I fight furiously to escape the dirt.

"Let me out of here, and I'll show you how well it will go for you all," I scream at her as she turns her back to me and walks away. I am left steeping in my raw feelings. How quickly this love has turned to hate. I let the pain swallow me whole and pour acid into my soul. The anguish marinates in me like scalding water as I stew in my own fury, staring at her back with fierceness. The GroundBreakers approach the raised prison they have formed for me and raise their hands in unison, lifting me off the ground and placing me on the platform. They plan to deliver me back to Naluen like this. It hits me that I have always been in a prison, one form or another, confined, restricted. A bird that desires freedom but flies out of its cage and straight into another.

"I won't be a prisoner again," I retort softly, defeated. I let my head hang and rest my chin on the soft dirt that surrounds me. Rage boils inside of me as I think of lifting my arms and setting this camp ablaze, sending the air around us crashing it into this group, letting the chaos take over and unleashing it into this world.

"I'm sorry, I really am. You're going to be safe and delivered back to Naluen. We are heading there now." She pats the packed dirt with her hands as she passes me, and I snarl and lash out, attempting to bite her hand. She draws it back immediately and looks at me wildly as she backs away into the tattered wagon. Fear crosses her eyes as she looks back at me, mounted on top of the platform.

I look up to the sky, tears still staining my face and burning my eyes. As I cry out, the sobs take me over. I hear the lash of a whip as the platform begins to move amongst the rocky terrain.

As we rock along down the freshly made road for what seems like forever, I give in to exhaustion. I think back to Nora and Commander Kirk at the Summer Palace when I was young. How I miss the warmth of their embraces and the smells coming from the kitchen, fresh bread, and apple pie. In my mind, I picture the warm bread coming out of the oven and Nora yelling at Lilliana, Anna, and me as she tells us not to touch it until it cools. We would always sneak away with pieces in our dresses and giggle as we tossed the hot bread into our mouths and made "huff huff huff" sounds at each other.

A rock catches the wheel of the wagon and brings me slamming back down into reality, still imprisoned in the ball of mud, still riding on the platform for all the forest animals to see. I continue to look out at the views of the Tangled Forest as we pass outlooks. I'm staggered by the beauty of the orange hues that deepen as they come up from the north. It's the most gorgeous thing I have ever seen, I think to myself, remembering to close my mouth. Neither the walls of the Summer Palace nor the view from my chambers could not compare with this scenery. I stare out over the horizon as the golden light from the sun hits my face and warms my cheeks with its glow. I don't even realize that we have come to a full stop.

The man Jasmine called Commander Gavin approaches my rocky prison and informs the rest of the caravan that we will be camping here for the night. He yells to other soldiers to post lookouts for Nadeem trackers and WindBreakers that may be coming for me. I know the WindBreakers will be sending gusts through the forest to detect obstructions hoping to find encampments along the way. I look over my shoulder to see the others working on setting up a large tent, made from sheepskin, as they erect the poles in the middle and lay the mats out. I sigh with fatigue; dirt streaks my face as I am lifted and placed on the ground by the GroundBreakers.

"You will stay here for tonight. Gaze up at the stars if you have to," Commander Gavin says as he strolls away from me. Jasmine follows him, discussing something.

I overhear their plans to get back to Naluen safely by avoiding the west mountains. I am not familiar with the western geography, so I drift off. I attempt to connect with the ground again, listening to the hum of energy surrounding me and connect with it. I force it to pour into me, letting myself be absorbed by the flow from the prison surrounding me. As it vibrates, I command it to my will, forcing it to release me, a crack splits in the crust.

It's nightfall when the wind picks up. At first, I feel it
blowing against my face slightly, and the breeze is a relief
against my sunburned face. I'm exhausted from working away
at my prison of compact soil that envelopes me. I give myself a
break as the Groundbreakers move about around the camp. The
wind picks up as I feel the pour of energy in my bones, the way
the wind vibrates through the edges of the forest and hits me
with a force that I recognize. It's then that I feel myself starting
to roll backward, braced by the wind. The GroundBreakers
holding me together stirred around me as they felt it too,
something approaching from the forest.

WHOOSH, the rush hits the camp as two
WindBreakers sear through the air on gliders, spread like bird
wings on their back, and flatten the camp's tents. I smile
incredulously as I recognize them as Nadeem guards. My smile
disappears when I realize they intend to take me back to

Nadeem, where I will face the Marquess and the other Nobles. Struggling to get free, I wiggle back and forth, hoping to catch traction without breaking my neck in the process. I hear shouting from the Naluen soldiers as they run out and shoot missiles of carved ground at the WindBreakers in the sky.

Commander Gavin rushes from his tent and draws his sword. He is lifted up from the ground by a gust of wind that sends him towards me with frightening speed. The WindBreakers drop in a swoop to the ground, and the GroundBreakers holding me prisoner disperse into the trees. I feel the freedom I have so desperately craved embrace me as I force the prison around me outwards. It cracks and rips, sending fragments flying in all directions. My knees hit the ground as the soil crumbles around me. Relief fills me as I start to connect with the elements, a deep inhale that nourishes my soul. I look out at the chaos that is unfolding among the camp.

"We have located the Ornae," one of the WindBreaker shouts in a swooping motion as he approaches me. As I look up to him and reach out, I feel the terrain lift and pierce through him in sharp spikes as they rise from the ground. Blood splatters over my face. He coughs once and stares at me while I scream. I back away, led by instinct, and stare in awe of the WindBreaker, who has been severely mutilated by the rocky spikes that protrude from his abdomen. I feel myself embraced by someone, and I turn to look up; in horror. The arms of Commander Gavin surround me, and I feel the cold metallic sting of his sword across my neck.

Chapter 16

"Move, and you die," he whispers in my ear.

"Everyone lay down your arms and weapons!"

The chaos slows to an abrupt stop as he presses into me, a foot taller than me. He tightens his grip on my waist and presses his sword to my throat. The warm blood itches as it trickles down the nape of my neck into my stolen uniform. It's ruined anyway, I think, as I had ripped it on every branch and bush from here to the Summer Palace. I feel for my dagger through the slit of my dress. It seems they never removed it from my body when I was wrapped in my prison of mud and soil. I witness the WindBreakers lowering their hands as they approach us and kneel, the GroundBreakers pulling the rocky terrain around them and shackling their arms and legs together. They will not be able to Break with their movement restricted.

The other Naluen soldiers surround us, and I feel the eyes on me as they line up, lit from the moonlight and fires around us. I stare into each of their faces. It's then that I notice that I do not see Jasmine in the lineup. I would love for her to see the pain she has caused me, for the hurt to travel across her face as she sees what she has done. I think maybe that the truth is that she didn't care at all. She would not care what Naluen wanted me for, as she had to have known they would want me dead. Anger flushes my neck as I struggle against his hold.

"They think they can bully us! They think they can rule us as well. We won't allow it," he booms into the crowd of soldiers lined up around us.

"Kill the WindBreakers!" he shouts as two soldiers start forward and grab them by the hair on their heads, tilting them back, so they stare up at the night sky.

"No!" I scream as tears start to pour down my face. I know they have given their lives to find me. They are going to die, and there is nothing that I can do. I close my eyes as I know I will be able to feel when their hearts beat no more. I notice the beating repetition of the hearts surrounding me, even the one that holds me tightly against my will. I noticed a third one behind me as well. I don't have time to think as the sword across my neck moves, and I feel myself flinch, then am slammed to the ground. I look up to see the WindBreakers still alive, the soldiers holding their heads back, staring at Commander Gavin and Jasmine, swords at each other's chests. I reach for my dagger through the slit of my dress and move forward. As the point of the dagger presses against his back, he looks over his shoulder at me. Fear crosses his face as his eyes move back and forth.

"Traitorous bitch!" Commander Gavin spits at Jasmine.

"You said that she would be delivered back to Naluen, safely," Jasmine presses forward, her face expressionless as stone.

"Then you can die with her." He's swift as he reaches for her and they force each other back. The soldiers don't know

148

how to respond. They stare awkwardly at the Commander and Jasmine as they forcefully burst into each other. Swords clanging along the way, they swipe furiously at each other. I lunge forward towards the Commander's back, and he spins towards me, meeting my dagger with his sword. Jasmine knocks him backward, and I feel the ground thud when he hits it, vibrations sinking into me. I let the ground sing to me and push back, vibrating it under the Commanders' body, allowing it to consume him. He's trapped. Jasmine advances towards him, raising her sword level with his head.

"Get the WindBreakers!" she screams at me, knocking me back into reality.

"NO!" the Commander screams. The guards surrounding them attempt to challenge me. I'm ready for their embrace, slicing through them. My dagger sinks deep into the flesh of one of the guards, and I hear his grunt as he hits the ground. I twist as another one approaches, our metal clinking together as we reach each other. I jerk away from him in a twisting motion, my arms burning from the force he meets my

dagger with.

Dropping to the ground, I anticipate his next move and

send my dagger into his abdomen. Warmth covers my hands as

I feel the heartbeat inside him stop. The crimson pool collects

around us as he collapses, and I feel exhaustion taking over.

Two more guards press forward. I dive towards the

WindBreakers, crawling to reach them. I scream out as white-

hot pain runs across my scalp, my hair knotted in someone's

hand.

I lunge forward towards the WindBreakers and touch

their exposed shoulders. Energy surges through me, and wind

around us erupts as screams echo through the howls. The pain

in my head seizes as I feel bodies lifted by the wind and

striking the ground in the distance. The vortex expands,

howling as it circles me and the WindBreakers. I look at their

prisons spiking up from the ground, and it sends chills down

my spine. I wave my hand as the ground retreats, dissolving in the gust. I feel the surge of the wind grow more intense and the trees bending to my will in the distance. It's a deep breath that quenches every part of my soul. I can't let go of this; it tastes too good. I feel the big smile spread across my face as my view of the encampment warps around us.

I stop when I feel the WindBreakers drop beneath my touch. Both drained, their skin is ashen and faces horrifyingly hollow with wild-eyed terror. I flex my hands in exhilaration as the wind dies around us, and I stare around the camp at the damage that was done. The trees have been torn from the ground, roots exposed, and the only evidence of a camp's existence is the fragments of wood surrounding us. Many of the Naluen soldiers' bodies are scattered about, the survivors groaning in pain. Backing away from them, I scan the area until I find Jasmine. Blood streaking down her face and into her mouth, she crawls on the ground. I want to help her, but I am frozen by the disaster I have caused. Eventually I make my way towards her after processing the damage.

"Do you need help?" I reach towards her, but she brushes me off. Limping towards a mound in the ground. The Commander lays several feet away. I hear him growling as he lays in the dirt, unable to break free, staring up at the night sky.

"You betrayed me!" she screams at him and then says something else that I can't understand. Standing over him, she reaches for her sword and raises it; she lifts the sword and drives it through his stomach. "Now, you can't hurt anyone. Let's go, Em, we have a Prior to find."

Silence overtakes us as we leave the camp of chaos behind us. The horror that I caused flashes through my mind and lingers with fatigue. We continue to make our way down the path as we notice the sun coming up. I let Jasmine lean on my arm and assist her along for as long as I can bear. I know her foot still hurts. We decide to stop in a clearing next to a stream, the icy cold-water splashes as it navigates the curves through the trees. As we sit, I reach down and lift her foot for inspection, moving her olive-green uniform up her leg. Her ankle is swollen.

"What are you doing, and where did you get that stuff?" she asks suspiciously as I rustle through the bags for something to help with her pain.

"I stole it from the soldiers when they were lying around asleep."

She stares at me blankly for a moment, but I refuse to maintain eye contact with her. I help her lean against a large oak tree with nicotine-colored bark as she groans in pain. I look down at her and want to lash out and make her feel the pain she has put me through. Jasmine stares back up at me, reaches for the bottle I dug out of the soldier's bag, and lifts her shirt. It's a nasty gash the size of my hand and glows furiously red against her umber-toned skin.

"Why did you kill him?" I finally ask as she tends to her wound, wrapping a torn cloth around her waist tightly.

"Because he was going to kill you," she says flatly and stares at me, "and I swore to protect you. This wasn't supposed to happen."

"Yet you continued to lie to me and lead me into the enemy's trap." I retort quickly, moving away and letting her foot hit the ground. She whimpers as she lifts it up, and I pack up the items back into my bag. She groans as she attempts to rise from the ground, and I press her back down onto the tree.

"Don't get up yet. I'm not done."

"I didn't know they were going to hurt you. I thought they were going to offer you Asylum."

"I didn't need Asylum!" I scream more loudly than I intend to. "I needed freedom, and you took that from me." I point at her as the pain crosses her face, and it brings tears to both of our eyes.

"What do you think would have happened to you if you had stayed?" Jasmine follows my gaze as she lays back against the large tree, cradling her in its giant roots.

154

"I would have been locked up in the lower quarters, but I wouldn't be here in the forest, fighting for my life!" I remove my boots and plop down to the soft grass, stretching my legs in the process. Emotion finally overwhelms me as I let myself drown in its comfort.

"You're going to find out, so I might as well be the one to say it." She turns and looks at me directly, seriousness overtaking her beautiful features. "Em, do you know why—"

"Don't call me that!" I seethe through gritted teeth, tears overcoming me and running down my face. I rub the scratch on my neck where the sword had cut me.

Pity takes over Jasmine's face, and she resumes. "Do you know why there is no Voya?"

"They disappeared! They're gone, every one of them!" I scream as I wipe my tears on my uniform.

"No, no, they didn't." She moves closer to me, and I feel the heat of her. "Although the Nobles would love if that narrative continued and is believed by all."

I stare at her and wonder why she is doing this; why she feels the need to go through with this.

"They want to make sure they maintain power over the kingdom. Having a new Voya would not be good. They would have to give up their power and let the Voya rule."

"I understand the transition of power would be a difficult one. I don't understand what you're saying."

"They were going to kill you, Em!" she screams at me as her eyes fill with tears. "You were never going to be Voya. They were going to sacrifice you like they have been doing for hundreds of years."

Stunned, I stare at her and feel the truth in my gut like a rock I attempt to swallow. I feel the sickness as it marinates inside me, and I wretch it up. The bitter foam that lingers on my lips is sickly as it runs across the dirt surrounding me.

"I'm sorry. I'm so sorry, but I couldn't let that happen," Jasmine says, trembling as she reaches for me, and I flail back and forth, avoiding her touch. "I'm so sorry." Tears streak

down her face as she stands next to me.

Chapter 17

I stare at her as she sleeps. Her dark-hued braids have come undone completely, little hairs poking out in different directions. Dirt covers her face, and I think of how I must look, running my hands over my frizzy hair. I lay back, letting the grass catch me as I fall and stare up at the morning sky. It seems like it takes forever to lull myself to sleep and let the sun coat me in its crisp morning brightness. I shiver against the wind as it caresses me and listen to the song of the auburn leaves rustling against it. Rolling over, I notice Jasmine walking back to the spot where we collapsed after our escape, and I rise up to greet her. She smiles weakly at me and helps me up off the ground. I look down to notice an imprint of my body where the soil hugged me tightly and refused to let go.

"My head is ringing." I rub my forehead as I stand next to her, stretching. She offers me some bark to chew on, and I take it, thanking her. She proceeds to gather up our stuff and covers the area where we slept.

"We need to get going. Even though Commander Gavin is dead, the rest will come for us. The Naluen government won't stop until they have you". She begins to stomp eastward, the sun blinding us as we make our way. I listen to my stomach rumble reflexively, and I think of food, the sweet scent wafting its way from Nora's kitchen to my nose.

"We will eat soon, as soon as it's safe." She rubs my shoulder kindly and keeps us moving at a brisk pace.

"Safe. That is something I am not sure I have ever had the luxury of experiencing." I stare at the ground as the harsh reality hovers in the air after being spoken. Jasmine grabs my hand and squeezes it tightly.

"You're safe as long as you're with me." I squeeze her hand back appreciatively, but I know that it's not true in my heart. I look back at her. I notice her long black eyelashes as they curve outwards over her golden amber eyes. It's when I think of that, that the pain in my stomach worsens, the pain of the betrayal that lingers and hurts worse than any hunger can.

I trust no one.

"I still don't understand," I say as I think of completing the ritual and being the Voya. "I thought they would have to answer to me." I realize how naïve I sound as the words leave my lips.

"That was never going to happen, Em." She looks forward, keeping us on the right track, where I have no idea. I have forgotten where we are, and any hopes of finding the Prior are dwindling.

"What now, though? What if there is no Ornae to go through with the ritual?"

"We don't know. Naluen priests believe that the powers of the Breakers will weaken if you're not executed. They need you to die to keep up the status quo and keep the Breakers in Nadeem strong. Have you ever wondered why they are so much stronger in Nadeem? How they live so much longer than anyone else?"

"I had always thought it was because they were blessed with me and ruled by the Voya." I had heard things about Breaking being weak in the past years but never put much thought into it as I had no use of my abilities at the time. Now I understand that they are weakening because the last sacrifice happened so long ago.

"They also believe that if you aren't sacrificed, the Breaking inside you will become too much to handle. You saw how destructive your touch is when you grabbed the WindBreakers." I think back to the moment of euphoria as the wind had filled me like an inhale that satisfied every part of me. "When I saw you had no powers, I wasn't worried because I thought we had nothing to worry about. No Breaking, no problem. However, now I think the bottled-up energy inside you will devour you." Her fierce expression strikes me head-on as she stares at me.

As we make our camp for the evening, I notice the fear inside me, telling me its slick story of how I will be overcome with power. Now that I finally have it, it won't last. I push it deep down inside and take a deep breath, laying out the mat. I move the basket of berries that I picked on our way and pull the stems and leaves off them. I look over to Jasmine as she brings the sticks back from the woods and carries them. Her hair is re-braided and falls on her shoulders in a curving pattern. I love the way it spirals around her head and flows like tendrils, framing her face. She comes closer to the camp and smiles at me; I wave at her, and I hear something in the distance. I pop one of the berries in my mouth and taste the burst of magnificent sweetness enter my body.

"You have to try these. I found them over in the bush, and they seem to be safe. I've had a dozen," I say as I eat them by the handful.

"You better slow down, or your stomach is going to—"

I turn my back to her as I straighten everything out for her to sit next to me when I hear a thud.

"I'm fine! Don't worry about me," I say. When I turn around, I see it, the arrow sticking out of her forehead. I scream as she drops to her knees, the firewood hitting the ground in a tumble.

Chapter 18

I feel the heartbeats before I see them; I sense the blood rushing through their veins as they gather around us. I spot Commander Gavin first, dark burgundy blood spotting his stomach, as he lowers his crossbow and approaches us through the trees. I lunge for my sword, tears stinging my eyes as I carefully step backward towards Jasmine's limp body. I don't bother to look down at the horror I witnessed, keeping my eyes and sword, fully extended, on Commander Gavin. I pause to feel her heartbeat and sense it slowing itself, struggling to beat as it thumps once more.

The pain inside of me boils over, and I scream at them. "What do you want from us?"

"We want you, dear. You have no idea how much trouble you have caused by continuing to exist here in Nadeem." He strides forward as the rest of the soldiers pile out of the woods, some of them limping, and surround us. My hands start shaking as I take in the scene, I have already lost, but I am not going down without a fight.

"I don't even have control of my Breaking; I am no threat here in the Tangled Forest," I replied heavily.

"That's not good enough for us. We need your head on a spike. The Breakers of Nadeem have too much power. It's time to level the playing field," he states as he presses through the forest brush towards the clearing where Jasmine's body lays.

"Well, you can't have me!" I promise as I swing my sword in a dash as Jasmine had taught me in the garden. No one is going to save you. Strike fast and hard! She had not taken it easy on me, and I am grateful for that as I push forward. He isn't expecting the lunge, and, still holding his crossbow, which I was counting on, he stumbles back but not in time.

As I make contact with his side, I feel the warmth of his blood as it infiltrates the air with its metallic tone. He gasps, "Wretched bitch!" He spins wildly and pulls his sword from its sheath with a ring, and I am ready for him. I lean back, expecting his blow, and dive to the ground. I let my legs come around and take his legs out from underneath him. He falls hard on his back, still gripping his stomach and sides. I move towards him and feel the sword in my hands. I want to hurt him. I want to end him with everything I have in me as the hate seeps into my movements.

As I lift my sword, I feel the ground swallow my legs and the dirt rise. Not again. I twist and stomp as I call to it, letting its song sing to me. It won't listen this time. The GroundBreakers gathering behind me press forward. They can control it better than I can. I feel myself being swallowed once more as Commander Gavin looks up at me and smiles.

"You really thought you could take me on? Stupid girl." He lifts off the ground, dusting himself off, and approaches the spot where I am knee-deep in my soil prison. Sword still in my hand, I panic and swing it wildly at him. He avoids my swipes and snatches the sword from my hands in one press. He holds the sword to my stomach and inches closer, smiling smugly and looking into my eyes. The mud has now gripped half of me, up to my navel and consumes my arms at my wrist as I attempt to wiggle from its grasp.

"You're a pathetic excuse for an Ornae, you can't even overtake a couple of GroundBreakers." He laughs, and the others join in unison as they approach us.

"We will rip you into pieces and send your parts back to the Summer Palace to let the Nobles know who they are dealing with." He leans forward and whispers into my ear, "Just like we did those who came looking for our prisoners. Don't worry. I've kept your little maid comfortable in the meantime."

Rage rattles through me as I stare at him with all the hate I have been collecting.

"Don't you dare speak of her like that!" I threaten helplessly.

"We were aiming for you, of course, but you just wouldn't cooperate." He laughs mildly with a sickening smirk. "When she was the one that they returned with, I realized that I had to do the job myself."

A throat-thickening nausea fills me as I grasp the realization that Lilliana is still with them. The horrors she must have experienced, and I have not been able to save her. Now I will die here, and she will be a prisoner forever. As he presses forward, his sword reaches my gut. I look over to Jasmine's limp body lying on the ground, and the thought of joining her hits me like a cold chill.

"Aw, it seems we touched a nerve. Well, you will be with her soon enough." He wipes my bangs from my face, and I stare directly into his face. I won't cry now; I won't let them see me cower in fear.

I raise my head, "I am the Ornae and the future Voya of Nadeem. I will not bend to your will."

I knew he meant to kill me, but I still gasp in awe as I feel the heat from my own sword slice through my stomach. I feel the strange vibration come to me as the sword enters my body. The song pours into me stronger than ever, fueled by my grief and hate. The pain sears white-hot as it rips into my flesh and sticks in the prison that surrounds my waist. He lets the sword hang there as he begins to walk away back to his camp. My body aches with the pain as I scream out into the air, gritting my teeth harder, and the song continues pouring into me as it overflows. I can't stop it. My own heart beats at a pace that scares me, and the vibrations increase the pressure building inside of me tenfold. The agony continues until I feel myself ripping at the seams, the sword in my stomach forgotten about, as the anguish leaves my mouth in a curdling scream. BOOM! It shoots out like a shockwave ripping through the air and landscape, causing the birds to take flight in the distance.

I am freed from my prison, commanding the ground to dissolve in a dusty whisp, the wind caressing mc off the ground. I'm lifted to see the soldiers staring up at me with their weapons and hands held up in defense. Commander Gavin turns towards me as he readies his crossbow and takes aim. I swipe the arrows from the air as they shoot towards me, and I pull the sword from my stomach. I swing it in a swiping motion and send it sailing towards a soldier, impaling him and pinning him to the tree behind him.

The rush of the elements answers my call as more of them surround me, pouring into me with a song that I crave so deeply. The wind encases my body in a protective shroud, and the soil rips forward and reaches for me. The water from nearby streams ripples across the ground coming to me as I call it forward in a rush. The water crashes into the soldiers and swirls around them at my command. I let it devour them as they writhe for freedom and air, succumbing to the unnatural current.

170

The heat licks up my arm as I feel it settling, and flames appear on either side of them, readying themselves for action. I dismiss the water as I hover above the crowd, the wind howling in my ears as its fury is unleashed, and it sends the men sprawling. Commander Gavin smacks the trunk of a tree with a sickening crack that feeds my want for more. The wind tears into his flesh and rips it from his body as I breathe deeply. I reach and feel the heartbeats of each of the men below me, some stopping and some beating so rapidly that I can taste the fear that overcomes them. I reach out to them and grasp them in my hands, the entire clearing stills as I listen softly to the beats as they gather in unison.

"You all took everything from me, and you will pay!" I swear dryly to the wind as tears streak my face. With a deep inhale, I think back on my times with Lilliana, us both snatching freshly baked rolls from Nora's kitchen and the smell of soup wafting its way into our noses. My insides turn molten as I recall us cuddling up by the fire after we just escaped a torrential downpour from the gardens, both soaked to our skin.

I fast forward to Jasmine, the training we were able to keep secret in the garden, and the bruises I had gained. With a smooth motion, I remember from Commander Kirk. I hold each of their hearts in my hands. The beating rings through me in unison as I feel each of them. I grab hold of them and rip. One by one, their screams fill the air until they each drop into silence. Tightening my fist until my white knuckles burn with satisfaction.

The soldiers collapse to the ground, their lifeless bodies decorate the clearing. I attempt to pull more, but the energy I so desperately crave flees my grasp. I struggle to hold on to it, to draw more of it from the elements around me, but it won't give. I have taken more than I should have. My gut twists in agony, and before I faint, I feel the impact of my body hit the ground. Dazed, I look up at the sky and feel my body being pulled, grass and twigs scraping my back as it grates across the floor of the Tangled Forest.

Chapter 19

A rocking motion startles me awake, and I feel nausea seep in with the swaying motion of the wagon. Dazed, I attempt to sit up, and feel hands holding me back down against the wooden floor. Its sharp edges cut into my back as I groan and lay back into it.

"Don't try and get up, Em." It's a voice that I recognize. Jasmine.

I am so confused that I just lay there and stare at her, assuming it's a dream. I look around for Lilliana, still on the floor of the wagon. If I am dead, they should both be here with me. I notice another man but move my eyes back to Jasmine and olive-green combat uniform, still covered in dirt and stains from the Tangled Forest. I immediately look to her forehead, nothing. Her umber, golden-toned skin glows in the light coming in the wagon window, and I cherish its sight.

"Impossible," I say, letting the tears roll down each side of my face. "I thought you were dead!" My voice is raw and hoarse as she wipes the tears from my eyes. They burn as they blur my vision.

"They are going to have to try harder than that. Good thing they didn't cut off my head." She stares back at Emma rubbing her forehead anxiously. "It took a lot longer to heal this time for some reason. When I woke, I saw the devastation of what had been done. I for sure thought that you were dead. I couldn't believe it." She stares at me seriously, and I can see the look of worry in her eyes.

"Me either," I choke out hoarsely.

"When I saw your body hit the ground, I knew I had to get you to safety. Luckily I had some help." Jasmine nods next to her, and I glance over at the other figure sitting beside her. An aged man with a long gray beard, who stares directly at me with a cold gaze. The song inside of me burns to my core, and it makes me scream out in pain.

"I apologize, child. I just didn't believe it." He rubs his chin slightly as he pulls back his hood, revealing an aged man with ivory skin, pocked with the kisses of the sun. He reaches out for me, and I lean back slightly. Jasmine rubs my shoulder soothingly and motions for him to lean back as she moves to the other side of me.

"I guess I should introduce myself." He shuffles closer, moving his hand outside of his robe and extending it towards me. "Hello Emma, I am the Prior."

The End

Notes

I hope you have enjoyed reading this book as much I have enjoyed writing it. Throughout my journey of reading books I struggled to find the story that fulfilled everything that I had wanted to read. We need more LGBTQ+ representations in media and writing and I wanted to contribute to that.

A huge thank you to my beta reader Alli, my editors Kennedy and Fay, and my proofreader Katie.

Warmly,

Tristen Davis

Made in the USA
Monee, IL
11 June 2022

97838731R00104